Puck the Halls

Book 7.5 in The Playmakers Series®

BY G.K. BRADY

ISBN 978-1-7363606-8-2

Cover design by Jenny Quinlan, Historical Editorial
Edited by Jenny Quinlan, Historical Editorial
Proofread by Word Servings
Printed in the United States of America
Trefoil Publishing

Contents

Dedication

To the men and women of Search and Rescue, who brave the worst Mother Nature can throw at them as they race against time to find those who need them most. How fortunate we are that this is their calling.

Chapter 1

BECKETT AND PAIGE

*B*eckett Miller guided the Escalade toward the highway, away from his mountain vacation house, his heart in his throat. Mere moments before, he'd been ecstatic at the chance to spend some much-needed alone time with his wife, but her sniffles from the passenger seat had sent his elation crashing into the floorboards.

He pulled in a silent breath. "The girls will be fine, Andie." She was Paige to everyone else—Paige Anderson Miller—but she'd been Andie to him since he'd known her in college. One of his pet names for her. But pet names and a soothing tone were doing little to slow her soft sobs, so he tried a different tack. "Did you see how excited the girls were when Grandma and Grandpa opened the door? Not to mention they get to spend time with all those other kids."

"I know, Beck, but the babies!" Andie's quavering voice about undid him.

Visions had been dancing in his head of peeling filmy bits of lingerie off his wife's luscious curves as soon as he got her into the mansion where they were staying for the next three days. Right now those pictures seemed as fictional as the sugar plums traipsing through little kids' dreams on Christmas Eve—which was a mere eleven days away.

Spotting a gravel turnout, he eased the SUV off the road and shifted it into park.

Andie stared at him with wide, watery eyes. "Wh-what are you doing?"

He stared back into their pale green depths, depths that brought to mind the shimmering geyser pools at Yellowstone. He often got lost in those eyes, like he was tempted to do right now, but he kept himself firmly planted in the driver's seat, brushing his fingers through her silky cinnamon strands. "I'm pulling over so we can talk about this before we get too far down the road." The "girls" were a sum total of four: elementary-aged Elayne, preschooler Audrey, and their nine-month-old twins.

Andie blinked, sniffled once, and gaped at him. "You mean you're willing to go back and get them?"

Not really, but if you think I am, maybe I can pull a rabbit out of my hat and nip this looming disaster in the bud. "I am, but first I want to point out that the bride and groom said adults only. I also want to remind you how long it's been since we've had a night alone. It's nearly Christmas, and we haven't had a date night since August. And not just alone in our bedroom twenty feet from the girls' rooms. *And* let me also remind you how long it's been since we've had a few days to enjoy uninterrupted conversations with other adults, eat adult food, and drink adult beverages without worrying about the consequences."

They were on their way to a different mountain getaway about twenty-five miles distant to celebrate a Christmastime wedding between their friends Blake Barrett, a Blizzard hockey player, and Michaela Wagner, Andie's real estate attorney. A mini-vacation at a Colorado castle they'd both been anxious for at one point, although now it appeared he was the only one still looking forward to it.

"I know, but—" she hiccupped.

"And how long have my parents been begging for time on their own with the girls?"

Andie cleared her throat, and a ripple moved through the creamy column of her neck.

"Since Elayne was born," he murmured, wrapping his fingers around her nape. "The girls have the best babysitters in the world, and they're in a house full of other grandparents and kids. Santa's taking time off from his workshop to stop by and see them. They couldn't stop talking about his visit and the giant sleepover, and they're not gonna be real happy with us if we yank them away from all that fun to bring them to a *boring* adults-only party." *Not to mention we'll be at the top of our friends' shit lists.*

"I know, but—"

She gripped her hands tightly in her lap, and he loosened one and dropped kisses on her knuckles. "You can check up on the girls anytime you want, and if anything happens, we're not that far. You said you were looking forward to spending time away, especially at this castle you helped Blake pick out. Has that changed?"

"No, but I ..."

He touched his forehead to hers. "Then what's the problem, pixie?" *Tell me so I can fix it.*

Her face crumpled, and fresh tears spilled down her cheeks, sending all his systems into five-alarm-fire mode. "I feel like I'm being a bad mom."

He reared back. "Why? How could you be a bad mom? Because you're getting away for a few days with your children's neglected father?"

Her phone pinged—it always pinged—and he was floored and a little pissed off when she held up a finger. "Sorry, it's the office. This'll only take a minute."

He watched as she typed out a text, then another and another. *Yep, neglected sums it up.*

She put the phone down. "Done. Now what were we talking about?"

3

He kept the eye-roll to himself. "Me being neglected and you being a bad mom."

She bobbed her head. "Leaving them, having fun without them, feels selfish." Another round of tears welled and beaded her dark lower lashes. "And now I feel like a bad wife because I have a neglected husband."

Darting his eyes to the sunroof, he expelled a sigh and leveled his gaze back on hers. The past week of coaching had been grueling, with the team losing several crucial games. Didn't help that Andie had missed nearly an entire game because of—what else?—work. He was only in his sophomore season, and his thoughts were often consumed with whether he'd be back to coach a third year. Would they can his ass? And if they did, then what? He *loved* coaching the DU Pioneers hockey team, the team he'd played for prior to turning pro, and it had nothing to do with earning money. But could he talk to her about this shit? Not when she was too busy taking calls.

The coaching position ticked so damn many boxes on his list of career must-haves, like placing him in the thick of a sport he loved almost as much as he loved Andie and the girls. Sure, his account balances said he didn't have to work, but he *needed* to work for his sanity. He'd been a little lost before taking the position; retirement was not a good fit for a guy like him. At. All. So yeah, money was not the be-all, end-all. He'd managed to rebuild a small fortune from the ashes of his career, and his wife also raked in buckets of money ... which led him to the uncomfortable yet familiar thought that in order to stay on top of her game, she was a career woman first, mom second, and a wife third. While she might argue the order of her priorities was reversed and that he was skewing things according to his personal filters, that was how he saw it. And he didn't like it.

Between her tears, the direction their discussion was taking, and the conversations inside his own head, his mental capacity was quickly draining. Did he have the reserves to understand and negotiate the whirlpool of emotions currently churning inside her? And why did she pick *now* to melt down? Couldn't she have done it when Blake and Michaela had first asked them to attend their wedding getaway sans kids? Andie had known what they were getting into back then, and she had wholeheartedly agreed.

Jesus, he'd been so focused on getting away, on getting a little touch time with her, that he couldn't wrestle back his disappointment. Andie's enthusiasm for the adventure had gone missing, and his chest deflated. If he were honest, *he* was being selfish. He wanted her unfocused attention on *him* for a change. Not on the kids, not on her business. Back on him, like it used to be. "It's not selfish," he finally replied, blanking on the exact reasons why.

Silence hung heavy in the air for several beats.

"It's not a long drive, Andie. Why don't we at least go and check this place out? Can you stand to be away from the girls for a half hour?" The last bit came out a little sharper than he intended—not that he hadn't felt the edge, but he wished he hadn't let his frustration leak into his voice.

She flicked a finger toward the windshield and grumbled, "Yeah, go." Then she folded in around herself and turned her face from him, but not before he caught her bleak expression.

Great. A fan-fucking-tastic start to the weekend.

Paige slumped in her seat, staring at an endless blur of flocked evergreens through the passenger-side window. Her mind whizzed like the passing scenery. Of all the ways she'd imagined starting their adult getaway, this inauspicious beginning hadn't made the list. Instead of laughing and unwinding, she was fighting fresh tears and her insides were wound as tight as a gymnast's bun. One glimpse at Beckett's glower told her that while he might not be holding back waterworks the way she was, he was as tense as she was. Clearly *not* a happy camper. Why couldn't he simply accept her reluctance to leave the girls without getting all huffy about it? It was bad enough her booming business pulled her away from them. The twins were only nine months old, for God's sake! She still had the baby fat hanging around her middle to prove it.

He was acting as if she had suggested they not join the other couples at the luxury mansion she'd been eager to help Blake find. Of course she wanted to go! When was the last time she and Beckett had cut loose with other couples without worrying about waking the kids or staying sober in case of midnight crying jags? Ages ago. Couldn't he see that, in spite of her niggling guilt, she wanted to go? Ever since Blake and Michaela had announced their last-minute wedding plans, she'd been pumped. Three nights in secluded mountain bliss? Who *wouldn't* want that? She'd even packed the lingerie her husband kept buying her that she had yet to model for him. She hadn't even removed the tags yet!

The thought of donning the sheer bits sent a jolt of fear streaking through her. Maybe if they kept the lights *real* low or turned them off completely, he wouldn't notice her extra-large grab bars. That assumed, of course, that this thundercloud sitting between them lifted before seduction time was set to begin. And darn, it needed to be early because she was exhausted!

Dinner at seven, between the sheets at eight, asleep by nine. Yeah, chica, *you are one sexy siren.*

Ugh!

And when would they fit in a call to the girls? Between the end of dinner and the start of romance. Fifteen minutes on the phone, forty-five minutes for making love. Plenty of time.

Did they need the call? The girls were in great hands. Heck, their mountain house was full to the brim with not only Beck's family, but the parents of nearly every Blizzard player attending the whirlwind wedding. The adults outnumbered the kids, and grandparents and grandchildren were equally excited about the fun they had in store.

She stole a quick glance at Beckett's profile as he commanded the steering wheel. His light brown hair was neatly groomed, his blue eyes were glued to the road, and his dark scruff was starting to show. He'd pushed his cuffs to his elbows, exposing powerful forearms crisscrossed with those man veins she loved to gawk at. Coaching kept his body ripped, and her eyes wandered to where his knit shirt clung to a flat stomach made up of a hard six-pack. Good thing she was seated because her knees had taken on the consistency of gelatin. The man was gorgeous. How had she lucked out? She'd never been that attractive to begin with, but right now she was in the running for the Frump of the Year award. Her busy work life left little time for pampering and prettifying—not to mention toning and tweaking. Did he notice how far from supermodel perfection she was? Probably. Did her appearance turn him off? Possibly. Not long ago, he hadn't been able to keep his hands off her, but now he seemed to have no problem keeping his body apart from hers. Where they used to make love four or five times a week, it wasn't uncommon to skip a week or two now and again. When was the last time he'd pulled her down in his lap or feathered kisses along her neck while she did dishes, growling that he needed her? For months now, whenever she came to bed after finishing up work in her home office, he was already sound asleep. And who could blame him?

His appeal hadn't slacked off in the least. That was true for not only her, but for the countless attractive women who blatantly admired him whenever he walked into a room. Her mind leapt to him picking one to drape over his arm, leaving plain Paige behind with four little girls while he cavorted among goddesses.

Stop it!

Oh God, she was doing it, wasn't she? Letting old insecurities overwhelm her, indulging in a good old-fashioned pity party for one. She needed to corral those feelings of inadequacy, but somehow she couldn't muster the energy.

"We're here," he announced as he turned onto a private road that wound through stands of aspens and pines. He gave her a sidelong glance, a smile tugging one corner of his mouth.

She blinked and looked around. A thick blanket of unmarked snow sparkled with the winter sun's golden rays. A few more curves and the scene before them opened into a meadow with a slight rise. Atop the slope sat a timber-and-stone building so large it could have been a hotel.

"Wow! This is beautiful." Her eyes widened as she took in the sight.

"Yeah, pixie. You done good. I think there will be plenty of room for all of us."

The Escalade's tires crunched over a wide gravel drive, and Beckett coasted it to a stop in front of a pair of oak doors carved with elk drinking from a river that wound through mountains.

"Wow!" she repeated, scanning the three-story building soaring in front of them. She swiveled her head side to side. "Guess we're the first ones here."

Beckett flung open his door. "Looks like. Let's check it out. You got the key?"

She opened her own door and stepped out, trying not to read too much into the fact he hadn't opened her car door in ... forever. Okay. So only twice in the past month, not that she was counting.

"Combo lock." She strode to the front door, ignoring him as well as she could ignore a man a foot taller and broader than she was, and punched in the code. A whirring sounded, then a click, and she gripped the latch. She swung the front door open, stepped inside ... and gasped. As a real estate pro, she'd seen a lot of stunning homes, but this one literally stole her breath. Standing in a foyer that soared at least thirty feet, she executed a slow twirl, taking in the stained-glass dome topping the space, rounded plaster walls, and marble floors inset with a compass. The space was decked out in fresh evergreen garlands woven with gold-and-silver ribbon and white lights.

Wow!

Beckett's eyes flicked to the design on the floor. "Huh. Guess we'll always know which way is north."

Delighted with each corner she turned and each room she peeked into, all of them equally festooned in holiday finery, she prowled the house, and he followed. When they eventually entered the last wing that housed several large master suites, he pointed at one that offered a floor-to-ceiling view of the Gore Range. "How about if we claim this room for ourselves? After all, you helped find the place, and we're the first ones here."

Every suite was a stunner suitable for royalty, though the one they stood in was definitely a notch above, and she should have left it for a different guest. But when she took in the hopeful expression on Beckett's handsome face, her inner good girl—the one who called her selfish—agreed. "Works for me."

He ambled toward her, his sizable eyebrows waggling. Reaching out, he slid a hand around her waist, dropped it to her ass, and squeezed. "How about we test out the bed to be sure it'll hold us for our upcoming, ah, activities?"

"What, now?" A laugh burst from her, and she gave his chest a little shove before she realized what she was doing.

He pulled back, his playful expression replaced by the same glower he'd sported in the SUV. "Guess not."

She forced out a laugh. "I was kidding!"

"Kinda like you were kidding when you promised to show up for my game the other night?"

What? "What do you mean? I was there."

"Being there, in your seat, and actually paying attention is a far cry from being in the building and doing business the entire time." His voice was an accusing growl.

A breathless moment later, she stood frozen in place, watching his retreating back as he muttered, "I'll get our bags."

Putting aside her bewilderment over his remark about her attending his game, she started to call out, "Wait! I didn't mean it the way it sounded," except she *had* meant it. It had been her first reaction to his playful advance, her natural reaction. Dear God, why had she responded that way? And why was the intimacy that had once been so spontaneous, so natural, all of a sudden such a difficult state to come by?

9

Chapter 2

T.J. AND NATALIE

Natalie Shanstrom was running out of time. For the entire drive from Denver to the mountain getaway where they'd spend the next few days among friends, she'd been working up the courage to start a familiar conversation with her husband. Familiar, yet uncomfortable and daunting. She darted her eyes to him, taking in his large, relaxed frame in the driver's seat of the Audi A8. An old tune, "Can't Fight This Feeling" by REO Speedwagon, warbled from the throwback station T.J. had tuned in, and he hummed along.

He threw her a sidelong glance. "You keep looking at me like you've got something on your mind, sweetheart. Am I driving too fast?" A wry grin tugged his generous mouth. His speed behind the wheel—or her lack thereof—was a typical topic between them, though more an inside joke than a serious discussion. Unlike the one hanging over her head like the proverbial Poe pendulum.

Her man was a serious badass on the ice, sending quivers of fear through his opponents. But with her, the badass became as soft and cuddly as a wiggly puppy, from his toes to the curly dark hair on top of his head. She was counting on that puppy as she blurted, "We should have taken the dogs to stay with the kids and the grandparents at the Millers' mountain place." They had two dogs, Ford and Deke, that they loved liked babies. But a hole had been growing inside Natalie that couldn't be filled by their canine children, no matter how much she loved them.

T.J. frowned and shot her another side-eye. "Why? It sounds like the place is going to be pretty chaotic. I don't think the elderly babysitters need a pair of dogs in the mix."

"Yeah, but still. Think how the kids would love having the dogs, and the dogs ... Oh my God! They'd be in doggie heaven licking all of those little faces." She paused to pull in a breath. "Dogs and children. Kind of a perfect pairing, don't you think?"

"I think all those hyped-up, grabby kids would freak the dogs the hell out." T.J.'s hand shot to the back of his neck and rubbed—his *tell* that he didn't like the direction she was trying to maneuver the conversation. His next words confirmed his silent signal. "Nat, if this is your way of bringing up the kid discussion again, I'm not sure I like it."

Yep, and there it was.

"It's ... I ..." She cleared her throat and got her pounding pulse under control. "Then when *is* a good time to talk about it, T.J.?"

"How about never?" he snapped.

Reflexively, she cinched her arms across her chest and ground her molars together to keep her mouth shut. Anything that came out of it would be raw, unfiltered, and very possibly regrettable.

After several charged moments that felt like hours, T.J. sighed. "Nat, we *have* talked about this. Over and over and over." He rolled his hand for dramatic effect, and she wanted to slap him. "You know how I feel about having kids."

"But when we got married, you said you were open to it," she accused. "Now it's always a nonstarter."

He expelled another breath. "Do we have to talk about it right before a fun weekend we've been looking forward to? Christ, we'll be there in fifteen minutes. This is hardly the time—"

"That's my point! There's *never* a good time."

He turned to glare at her before leveling his gorgeous hazel eyes back on the road. "Are you *trying* to ruin our mini-vacation before it even starts?"

With a huff, she sank into her seat. "God, you are such a jerk sometimes!"

"That's not what you said last night," he quipped. "As I recall, after orgasm number three, you were screaming that I was a fucking god. Pretty sure the neighbors heard you."

"Don't even! You're not taking this seriously!"

"Oh, I take delivering every orgasm *very* seriously."

The navigator interrupted with instructions to turn onto a private road, and Natalie turned her glower to the scenery outside the passenger window.

When T.J. spoke again, the cockiness was missing from his tone. "We have a good thing going, Nat. Why ruin it by having kids right now? Besides, we're both still young. We have plenty of time."

His trite words had her sitting ramrod straight. God, she'd heard this same argument so many times before, and she was sick of it. Between clenched teeth, she hurled back a few worn words of her own. "No, we don't. Not if we're going to have more than one. And you're just doing what you always do, which is kicking the can down the road. You're going to kick it so far that time will run out. At least for me it will," she grumbled. "If you decide to have kids forty years from now, all you need is a willing twenty-something, and poof! You're a dad. I don't have that option."

He slowed the vehicle to a crawl and gaped at her. "If I don't want kids now, why the hell would I want them when I'm in my seventies?"

"So now you admit you don't want kids!" She glared daggers at him, and he had the decency to suck in a contrite breath.

"I didn't mean it like that," he backpedaled. Foot depressing the accelerator once more, he lurched the Audi forward. "Nat, you just don't get it." His soothing tone chafed at her like a coarse tag in a blouse. "After the crap childhood I had, I'm not very promising dad material. Who's to say I won't be just like my father was? Is *that* what you want for your children?"

Now it was her turn to gape. "T.J. Shanstrom, you know that's not true! Look how you are with the dogs. Look how you are with me. How you are with your teammates' kids and the tiny fans who swarm you constantly! And look at your sister. She went through the same awful childhood, but she turned it around. Your nephews are incredible. Don't you want kids like them someday?"

He pulled the car to a stop and pointed at the windshield. "We're here."

We're nowhere.

She'd been so caught up, so frustrated by their growing insoluble debate, that she hadn't noticed the colossal structure blotting out the sky in front of them. Not until T.J. cut the engine and opened his door did she take an appraising look at their home away from home for the next few days. "Oh my God, this place is huge! And beautiful!"

"Paige really outdid herself," he agreed as he prepared to shut his door.

The movement startled her back to their conversation—such as it was. "T.J., where are you going? We're not done."

"We are for now, Amber Eyes." He lifted his chin toward the massive front door. "Hey, Millsy. Quite the place, huh?"

Natalie turned to see Beckett trundling down a short flight of stone steps suitable for a French country estate. Damn! T.J. had slipped his hook *again*. He'd gotten really good at diversion and avoidance whenever the subject of children came up. Beckett flashed her a smile and headed for her door. Only then did T.J. close his and hustle around the hood to open her door for her.

"I got this," he barked at his friend.

Beckett threw his hands up and backed off. "I got you, bro. Didn't mean to threaten your door-opening prowess. You were a little slow on the uptake, and I just wanted to make sure Natalie didn't get left behind."

She opened her own damn door, thank you very much, and vaulted from her seat to give Beckett a hug. "Thank you, Beck.

Always nice to have a gentleman looking out for me. Paige inside?"

"Yep. She was scoping out the kitchen last I saw."

Without a backward look, Natalie made for the front door. With any luck, Paige had rented a place that offered extra bedrooms.

Because I am not about to share one with your slippery ass, Tyler Johnson.

T.J. blew out a breath and smoothed the hair at his nape. He'd dodged a familiar bullet ... or had he? As he watched his wife's shapely, jean-clad ass swaying up the stairs, it occurred to him he might have been as close to that swell—and every other body part belonging to her—as he was going to get for the rest of the getaway. Natalie was right, of course, that he'd promised kids were in their future when she'd agreed to marry him. It had been one of her conditions, and he'd gone along willingly. Hell, he'd have walked across hot coals a hundred times over to be with her; agreeing to kids had been a no-brainer. Whatever she wanted. But now? When life was sweet the way it was and everything between them was so perfect? Bringing kids into the mix could fuck it all up.

A disturbing thought rocketed through his brain. *It may be perfect now, but it's not going to stay that way.* Her offhanded remark about him having kids with someone old enough to be his granddaughter had been almost laughable, except it had jolted him to the realization that if Natalie got tired enough of *his* bullshit, she could go find a twenty-something of her own *right now* who'd be more than willing to deposit his sperm into her body and give her those kids she wanted so much.

Picturing her with another man, her long dark hair sweeping like a curtain over his bare shoulders while he looked into those coppery-gold eyes of hers, rousted old Spiky Green from hibernation deep in his gut. In his frustration, he growled at

Beckett. "Thanks, asshole. Making me look bad in front of my wife."

"You don't need my help for that, dickwad," Miller chuffed. "Looks like you're perfectly capable on your own."

You have no idea.

They exchanged a quick bro hug. "Good to see you, man!" Miller exclaimed. "How about a brewski?"

"Sure. Lead the way."

Miller did—around the side of the house, to T.J.'s surprise—and stopped in front of a massive cooler on a patio the size of an ice rink. He fished out a few bottles, uncapped one, and handed it to T.J. before uncapping his own. "Cheers," he said as he clinked his bottle to T.J.'s

T.J. took a swig. Why were they standing out in the cold? "So I hear this is quite the place. Want to give me a tour?"

Miller took one long gulp. "Nah. Let's wait for the girls to look around first. Might take a while. In fact, why don't you and I head back out front and wait for the rest of the guys?"

Okaaaay. A little strange, but then again, it wouldn't hurt to let Nat cool off for a bit. Maybe with a few Crown Royals in her system, she'd relax and want to talk to him again ... about anything but the elephant taking up space between them. Yeah, that. T.J. was going to have to face the music sooner or later, but he'd opt for later.

He tugged his coat collar up around his neck and followed Miller to the front of the house.

Chapter 3

GAGE AND LILY

Gage Nelson opened the driver side door and waited for his wife, Lily, to slide behind the wheel before closing it. He strode to the other side and folded himself into the passenger seat. "Ready, Goldilocks?"

"Ready, Professor." She shot him a mischievous smile, her beautiful blue eyes sparkling like freshly polished sapphires.

His eyes grazed the Millers' mountain house, where they'd just dropped off their daughter, Daisy, their baby son, Brodie, and Lily's parents. He swiveled his head toward his wife. "You sure you're okay leaving them here?"

She started the engine and steered the white Range Rover down the driveway. "Who? The kids or my parents?" she laughed.

"Haha. The kids, of course."

"Absolutely. Besides my folks, did you see how many adults are there? And Aunt Ivy and Uncle Parker will be there tomorrow. This place is going to be rocking. By comparison, I think our little old rental castle will be pretty sedate."

"Oh, I don't know," he chuckled. "There's a bowling alley, an indoor pool, like three hot tubs, five bars, and fourteen adults ready for some hedonism."

Her eyes widened. "Are we talking orgies here?"

He barked a laugh. "No! I meant cutting loose, having a good time. The good times that involve sex will be restricted to each couple's suite ... or a hot tub. At least, I'm pretty sure that's the case. It's for damn sure the case where you and I are concerned."

Her head jerked toward him, her long golden curls dancing on her slight shoulders. "You don't think the others—"

"No, I don't. Eyes on the road, beautiful."

Her shoulders seemed to relax several inches. Turning her focus back to the driveway, she eased the SUV onto the road that led to the highway and their escape for the next few days. "Hmm. Sounds like someone is assuming there's going to be sex in our bedroom."

"Not assuming. Counting on it." He reached over and gave her knee a squeeze. "I'm thinking maybe I'll just strip you down, tie you to the bed, and keep you there the whole time." He waggled his eyebrows at her.

Her lips twitched. "Ooh, promises, promises, Professor."

Another chuckle rolled through him as he contemplated following through on the baseless threat his baser self was cheering for. His cock twitched its appreciation for the idea and the dirty scenes on his mind's movie screen. But it was time to turn from fantasy to reality, and he pulled out his phone with a sigh. The call he was about to make was the reason Lily was behind the wheel this time rather than him. He needed to gird himself mentally and fall back on every ounce of brain matter at his disposal.

Lily seemed to sense his reluctance, and she patted his thigh in a show of silent support.

He swiped his mother's number, and she picked up on the first ring. "Hello, Gage? Is that you?" Her voice rang through the car's speakers.

"Hi, Mom. It's me. How are you? How's Grandma?"

"I'm fine, and so's your grandmother. She's had a week of good days."

Thank God! His grandmother's dementia could swing from lost to lucid in the blink of an eye. "Good to hear. I'll give her a call." He breathed a little sigh of relief. Maybe this phone call would be easier than he had assumed.

That happy thought was crushed when his mother continued. "But what's this I hear about you leaving my grandson with Lily's parents? Why didn't I know about this? I would have flown out—on my own—to take care of Brodie." Her voice was strained, a mix of hurt and anger, a tone she had mastered over the years.

Fuck.

Fuck, fuck, fuck! How did she find out?

He exchanged a look with Lily, who rolled her eyes and mouthed, "What about Daisy?" No escaping the flicker of anger in those big blues. Daisy wasn't his by blood, but he'd adopted her after he and Lily married. On paper and in his heart, where it mattered most, Daisy was every bit his. Unfortunately, his mother didn't always concur. Then again, she still had trouble accepting Lily as her daughter-in-law. He and Lily enjoyed a mostly conflict-free marriage, but if there was one festering thorn, it was the one he was presently talking to. He was often stuck between a rock and a hard place without a means of easy escape.

Right now, though, leaving Daisy out of the conversation seemed the wisest course. "It was a last-minute thing, Mom. Our friends saw an opening in the game schedule and decided to take advantage, and they wanted us at their wedding. Didn't have a lot of time to plan."

"A break in the schedule, hey?" his mother huffed. "And you chose to party instead of coming to see your grandmother? She's not doing well, Gage."

The part his mother omitted, but that was laced throughout the guilt trip she was lobbing at him, was that he'd chosen not to plan every free day around coming to see her either.

"You just said she had a string of good days," he reminded her, biting back his defensive side that wanted to argue it was a wedding, not a party, a miniscule difference she wouldn't buy anyway.

"Well, yes, but who knows how long it will last? Sometimes I wonder about your priorities—"

"Mom, my priorities are right where they need to be. What I was trying to explain is that Lily's parents were already planning to come out for a visit, so they offered to take Daisy and Brodie." A stretch of the truth, but hey, it wasn't a total lie. They *had* planned to come out—they just hadn't decided when until he and Lily had hurriedly asked them. And asking *his* mother had never entered his mind. Well, maybe a glimmer of a thought had flared that he'd quickly squelched—and for good reason. His mother was all drama and guilt trips, while Lily's parents were as easygoing as she was.

He stole a glance at her. Her expression broadcast she wasn't feeling so easygoing listening to him talk to his mother.

"I would have flown out at the drop of a hat, Gage, and I wouldn't have even asked you to pay for it." Mom sniffed.

Gage dragged a hand across his jaw, calculating how to end this conversation. "I'm sorry it didn't work out this time, Mom. Next time something like this comes up, we'll—"

"Is it the money, Gage?"

"What?" Hadn't she just said she'd pay for her own way out? Not that he'd have gone for that. Of course he would have paid, and it wouldn't have been a problem.

"The money. You're getting older, and your coach isn't playing you on the first line consistently. Your career and those big paychecks won't last much longer. I hope you're socking money away, or is Lily spending it all on the fancy house and that wardrobe of hers?"

Her words slapped him on so many levels, setting different emotions to roiling inside his gut. One was abject misery. His play *had* been sliding, and there was always a younger guy ready to fill in. Yeah, he'd been worried about that. He was in the last year of his contract, and he had no idea where he'd end up in six months. The uncertainty and the thought of moving was akin to a rat nibbling at his toes. With a wife and kids and a home in

Denver he loved, how upended would their world be at the beginning of next season?

Two was panic, fierce and swift, spiking inside him at Lily's reaction to his mother's blatant show of dislike. It wouldn't be the first time wicked words sent his wife into a tailspin, not that he could blame her. In his peripheral vision, Lily's mouth dropped open. *Oh shit!*

"Excuse me?" she screeched before he could stop her.

On the other end, his mother gasped. "Gage! You didn't tell me we were on speaker! I thought we were having a private conversation!"

Was it too much for him to expect his mother to acknowledge Lily with a "hello"? Yep, it sure was. Not that a simple greeting could have defused this exploding shit-show.

"Mom, we're almost at our destination"—a total and complete fabrication because he had no earthly idea where the fuck they were—"so I need to go. I'll call you in a few days." Absently, he tossed out, "Love you," before disconnecting.

Wincing inside, he hazarded a look at Lily. Her delicate jaw was set in stone, and though her eyes looked straight ahead, he could tell from his vantage point that they blazed like flares.

"Lil—"

"Chickenshit!" she snarled.

Okay. He probably deserved that. "Goldi—"

"Oh no, no, no, Gage Nelson. I am *not* your Goldilocks. Not if you can't even stand up to your mother, who continues to do everything in her power to drive a wedge between us so she can see you married off to Jessica fucking Phelan!"

Not good. Lily was invoking the ghost of girlfriends past in Jessica, whom he'd *never* intended to marry and never would.

Yep, he was totally screwed. *Rock, meet hard place.*

"Lily, you know Mom. She ... she's ... she doesn't pull any punches."

Lily's head pivoted toward him once more, her eyes and mouth puck-round. "Are you saying there's validity to those awful things she just said about me?"

"Well, no, but she has a point about the house. I mean, to her it's an extravagance she probably can't comprehend and—" Lily swerved and he jerked, his stomach dropping somewhere around his ankles. "Road!" He flapped a finger at the windshield just as the nav system warned of a turn coming up.

Lily made the turn with a screech of the tires, then a slide as they bit into gravel. She slammed on the brakes, bringing the Range Rover to a jolting stop in the middle of the road. Throwing the vehicle into park, she proceeded to tumble out of the door.

"What are you doing?" he cried.

"You drive, Mr. Perfect!"

God, now he was juggling two drama queens! He stomped around the back of the SUV to avoid her stomping around the front. After adjusting the seat, he slid behind the wheel.

The inside of the vehicle was suddenly much warmer, and not in a good kind of way. Gage hit the gas, intent on getting to their destination so he could put breathing room between himself and his very hot—in every way imaginable—wife.

Oh. My. God! When will this end? Nola Nelson, I despise you more than I ever thought I could despise anyone! And, Gage Nelson, you'd better pick sides in this battle. Being a wafflemeister of epic proportions will not win you any awards!

Fuming, Lily yanked her arms across her chest and drilled holes into the side of her husband's head, trying to ignore his soft, neatly groomed golden-brown hair, trimmed brown beard, and impeccable body in unrumpled jeans and body-hugging ivory sweater. He was ... perfect. "Do you really think I spend too much?"

"No, of course not!"

"Then why didn't you tell *her* that?"

He let out a long, slow exhale and turned toward her, his eyebrows slashed over his crystal-clear eyes—one blue, one green. "She's my mom."

"And I'm your *wife*!"

His only answer was to glance out his driver's side window.

Agh! She'd been a little spendy lately. Had she overdone it? If she had, would he tell her, or would he simply let Nola fill his ear with how awful his wife was, then commiserate with the nasty woman afterward? Was he *worried* about money, about his financial future? His role on the team had been in flux, but he never talked about it. In fact, whenever Lily broached the subject, he brushed it away like an insignificant gnat. What about his future with the team? And didn't that affect her future and the kids' too? Did the question keep him up nights? No clue. If it bothered him, he obviously didn't want to talk about it, and she wouldn't be prying it out of him over the next few days.

Had he confided in his sister? Sarah Nelson would be here soon, along with her husband, Quinn Hadley, Gage's teammate and friend. Lily bit at a hangnail, turning over how she might prod Sarah without exposing their dirty laundry.

Though the silence in the Range Rover's cab stifled her into breathlessness and seemed to go on for days, they were pulling in front of the mansion—or castle, rather—within minutes of their last words to one another. Out front stood Beckett Miller and T.J. Shanstrom, sharing words over beer. When they spotted the Range Rover, they both beamed and waved. Gage beamed back, the most she'd seen his facial muscles move since their spat. After killing the engine, he sprang from the seat and headed toward the two men as if they were long-lost castaways, completely abandoning her in the passenger seat—not that she expected him to bow and scrape, but even a head bob her way would have been appreciated. Instead, she got Beckett Miller heading toward her, reaching for the door handle before she realized he was playing the gentleman—unlike her mother-loving husband.

"Hey, Lily!" Beckett practically dragged her from the car and gathered her up quickly in his substantial wingspan before releasing her. "The girls are inside checking out the place, if you want to join them. We'll get your bags."

"Thanks." She flicked her eyes toward Gage, but his back was to her as he talked animatedly with T.J.

Hmph. Tie me to the bed? Not on your life, Professor. You'll be lucky if I let you sleep in the same bed.

She flashed Beckett a dazzling smile before rushing off toward an impressive set of front doors. Inside, she was greeted by the musical sound of women's voices, and she wound her way through a maze of spaces until she reached the kitchen. Paige and Natalie turned and threw their arms wide, squealing her name as she rushed to them, as if they didn't see one another on a weekly basis. God, she loved her sistahs in crime and most everything else. Together, they all laughed—about what, she had no idea, nor did it matter—but it felt right to be here, among these women who shared the unique sisterhood of being with men who lived squarely in Not-Normal World. In other words, their husbands were gods to many but in truth were real flesh-and-blood men with imperfections. In this moment, some of those imperfections loomed larger than others in one particular man, but she shoved the thought aside.

Time to leave it behind and get down with the fun girl stuff!

She looked between Paige and Natalie. "Have you taken a tour of the place yet?"

They both nodded. Paige strode to an enclosed bar at one end of the kitchen. The space looked to be the size of an average bedroom and was stocked with brilliant cut-crystal glassware and bottles of all shapes and varieties that sparkled as though they had recently been buffed. Paige cocked an eyebrow. "And we're ready to show you around, but first how about a glass of your favorite white wine? This place is huge, and I highly recommend taking your cocktail to go. It might be a while before we make it back."

"Oh God, yes!" Lily enthused. A midafternoon glass of wine wasn't typically her thing, but today she'd make an exception. Maybe it would help her push down the leftover anger and guilt niggling at her.

"Speaking of which ..." Natalie picked up two short tumblers from a massive granite island. "How about I refill ours, Paige?" The glasses held ice and traces of brown liquid, and she rattled the cubes as she joined Paige.

"You read my mind, Nat." Paige pulled down a wine goblet and sent Natalie a wink. "Can I trade my husband in for you?"

Grinning, Natalie inspected a bottle of Crown Royal before tipping it into one of the glasses. "I'll take that trade. The thought of him and T.J. cuddling together is already making me giggle." She topped off the other glass from a bottle of top-shelf bourbon.

Paige poured a large measure of chilled white wine, offered it to Lily, and raised the glass Natalie had just handed her. "Woman power!"

They all yeah-yeahed and took healthy swallows.

Paige smacked her lips. "So good! How about after the tour, we get into our bathing suits and carry the party to one of the hot tubs? We'll turn it into our exclusive girls' club. No boys allowed."

"Yes!" Natalie cheered.

"First I need to find my room, then I need to get my bags."

"Tell Gage to put his worthless ass to work and bring them in. Chop, chop!" Natalie stuck her nose in the air and snapped her fingers before breaking into laughter. "Where is he anyway?"

"Being worthless with your two husbands," Lily quipped. "I'll get them myself." Giddiness had moved in and given glumness the boot, thanks to her friends.

"Oh no, you won't," Paige announced. She cupped her hand beside her mouth. "Justin? Oh, Justin!" she singsonged.

A good-looking guy in a tight black T-shirt and black jeans materialized from behind a wall on the opposite side of the kitchen. Wiry and well-defined, he broke into a brilliant smile that popped a dimple. "You sang, Miss Paige?"

"I did. Might one of your very capable staff be willing to liberate our friend's baggage from her vehicle so she can get settled in her quarters?" Paige gave the man a spectacular eyelash flutter.

Lily did a double-take. Had she slid between the pages of a Victorian novel?

Paige waved a graceful hand in their direction. "These are my friends and associates, Natalie Shanstrom and Lily Nelson. Friends, this is Justin, who is not only the concierge during our stay, but he's a chef whose amazing culinary skills are on par with no other."

Chef Justin executed an elegant bow, then covered his heart with his hand and locked dark eyes on Paige. "Your words fill my heart with joy, Miss Paige. I live to serve, as does my staff. As you wish."

After getting a description of the vehicle, he disappeared around the corner from where he'd first emerged, but his voice remained present as he barked orders to people obviously hidden from view.

"Isn't he great? I just love him," Paige giggled.

Natalie hmphed. "Does he come with the place?"

"No, I know him from Denver. I asked him to take care of us during our stay, and he agreed, which is lucky considering the Christmas crush. Kind of like having built-in hotel staff, huh?" Paige positively glowed with self-satisfaction, and Lily stifled a laugh.

"Might be something else going on there besides luck," Natalie scoffed. "I bet all you have to do is wave your pinkie, and he'll come running."

"Well, yeah. He's in the service industry," Paige pointed out. "Okay. Lily's bags are taken care of, so, ladies, we are off to discover!"

An hour later, Lily was seated in a steaming hot tub with Paige and Natalie, the bubbles soothing her frayed nerves into submission—her third glass of wine might have contributed too. Gabbing about one topic after another, sometimes giggling at utter nonsense, they managed to avoid talking about their husbands, for which she was infinitely grateful because it was a subject she needed a break from. One of Justin's staff, or Justin himself, seemed to always be nearby if a refill or a nosh was needed. Yessir, this right here was the escape she'd craved—the one she'd hoped to find with Gage—but damn it, she didn't need him around to have fun. Let him freeze his ass off with his friends, or wherever he was. *Probably on the phone with his mother.* Lily hadn't seen or spoken to him since they'd arrived, which was fine by her. *Ha! He can find his way to our suite without my help—or a map.*

And if he got lost along the way? She'd let Mr. Perfect figure that out just like he had everything *else* figured out. He was on his own.

Chapter 4

QUINN AND SARAH

S arah Nelson craned her head to get a better view of the estate unfolding through the windshield of her husband's Dodge Ram. She blinked.

Turning in the passenger seat, she faced his patrician profile. "Wow. Wonder if we have to cross a moat and pass through a portcullis to reach this place?"

Quinn Hadley gave her sidelong glance. "How many acres did Paige say this sits on?"

"A couple hundred? I think it also abuts a couple thousand acres of public land."

"Which is where we're snowmobiling tomorrow." Quinn snorted. "Still can't believe Barrett picked a snowmobiling trip for his bachelor party."

"Sounds fun to me—more fun than the girls' spa day Michaela planned." Sarah was more tomboy than girly-girl, and tearing around the woods on a speed machine held more appeal than getting herself buffed and polished.

Glancing down at her T-shirt, she smoothed a hand over a colorful cartoon Christmas tree. Beside it were two empty boxes labeled "Naughty" and "Nice," along with a third one that said, "I tried." That box held a check mark. She'd given Quinn his own Christmas T-shirt, and he'd indulged her by wearing it today. It featured a Santa holding a big candy cane alongside the words,

"It isn't going to lick itself." She took a moment to admire the way the black fabric molded itself to his carved musculature as she ran her gaze over her hunky husband. "You sound disappointed. Were you hoping for strippers instead?"

A slow, lazy smile spread over his handsome face. "Who says we're not getting strippers? Maybe they'll be waiting for us on the snowmobiles."

"Brrr. Sounds cold!" She exaggerated a shiver.

Quinn let out a chortle. "Yeah, might be tough stuffing bills into G-strings with icicle fingers. I don't think the strippers would like it much either."

Sarah barked a laugh. "Stuffing G-strings? In your dreams, Sparky!"

"Not *my* dreams, Sunshine. There's only one naked woman in my fantasies." He winked a cocoa-colored eye at her.

She tugged on a lock of his long brown hair. "That naked woman better be me."

He nodded. "She is."

Her eyes caught on a stone-and-timber structure coming fully into view. "This has got to be the place." *And it's beautiful!* "I can just make out my brother, T.J., and Beckett standing out front like a trio of doormen."

Quinn chuckled. "Eagle eye. Wonder what the hell those idiots are doing outside?"

"Drinking beer," Sarah replied dryly.

"But it's twenty fucking degrees!"

She shrugged. "Maybe they were being obnoxious and the women threw them out." She tossed him a grin. "Looks like I'll be staying warm on the inside, Sparky."

"And you'll be doing it with me, babe." He jabbed a thumb against his chest. "No way am I staying out in this weather longer than I have to, especially when my creative mind can invent way more fun things to do *inside* with you." He ducked his head. "Christ, this place is like a fucking palace!"

Sarah ran an appreciative gaze over the building's lines. "Sure is. It's even bigger than that behemoth you rented when we first got together."

He opened his mouth, but whatever he was going to say was cut off by an incoming call over the car's speakers. His index finger tapped the screen. "It's your mom."

"I don't want to talk to her right now!" she near-barked.

His eyes flicked to hers in question.

"She doesn't know we're here," Sarah explained, "and if she finds out, she'll get bent out of shape that she wasn't included."

One dark eyebrow dipped. "But these aren't her friends. How could she possibly expect to be invited?"

"It's not so much that she expects to be included in our social stuff, but she's been feeling neglected lately, and she'll resent the fact that Gage and I are getting together without her. *Especially* if she finds out Gage and Lily left the kids with Lily's parents." Sarah shuddered.

He pressed the red icon on the screen and continued his slow crawl toward the castle. "All right, but you're going to have to talk to her sometime so she doesn't blow up *my* phone."

"I will." A sigh whooshed from Sarah's lungs. "You know, she's still wondering if we're flying out to spend Christmas with her in the Bay Area or if she's flying in to stay with us."

He did a double-take. *Oh crap, here we go!* "Why? I thought you straightened her out. We're *not* flying out there, and I'm not flying her in to stay with us."

Sarah bit down on her thumb pad. "What if she flies herself in?" She didn't dare tell him her mother had already threatened to do just that.

"Sarah," he groaned, "please, for fuck's sake, tell me you didn't invite her. We agreed that if we were spending Christmas with anyone's parents, it was with mine—and only for a few hours, tops. Do you not remember having this same conversation already? Like, three times at least?"

She rolled her eyes. "Of course I do. But do you really want to leave either set of parents alone?"

29

"They're not alone," he argued. "I want to start our *own* traditions. Sweetheart, we've talked about this. I don't understand why the hell we're revisiting the same subject again." He came to a stop and threw the truck into park before killing the engine.

She puffed out a breath. "Okay. We'll talk about it later."

He swiveled his head and cut her a glare. "No, we won't. Babe, the subject is closed."

Before she could counter, her door flew open. Beckett leaned in and grinned. "Welcome to wedding central, kids."

Quinn stepped out of the truck. "What are you assholes doing out here?"

Beckett shrugged his big shoulders. "What does it look like we're doing? We're freezing our balls off. Come on and join us. We're having a competition to see whose will fall off first."

His back to her, Quinn headed toward the other two when Beckett offered her a hand. "The girls are inside doing God-knows-what."

"Staying warm probably," she quipped, though she didn't feel a single thread of humor in her being.

"No doubt," he snickered. "Just leave your bags. Someone will get them."

In her peripheral vision, Quinn was already tipping back a longneck, looking perfectly content with his friends. He didn't even give her a passing glance as she entered the mansion's soaring entryway. Spinning slowly, she took in beams and iron bands and trusses. A clearing throat made her jerk.

"Might you be Sarah?" a slight woman asked. Dressed in black slacks and black blouse topped with a red apron, she wore a tentative smile.

"I'm Sarah. How did you know?"

"The other ladies told me to be on the lookout for a, uh, festive T-shirt." The woman gestured. "If you're ready to join them, follow me. Right this way."

"I can find my way."

The woman let out a little laugh. "Possibly, though it'll be much quicker if I guide you there first."

They wove their way through a maze of halls and open rooms, and it struck Sarah she should be leaving a trail of crumbs. When the woman reached a set of French doors, she flung one open. "Just inside the gazebo there. May I get you a drink?"

Giggling and bubbles reached Sarah's ears. "Uh, a beer would be nice."

The woman nodded and retreated, and Sarah soon found herself beside a hot tub big enough for thirty people but holding only three. A foot kicked up out of the water, causing a splash. "Sarah!" Lily sang out. "You're here!" In one hand, she clutched a mostly empty wineglass.

"Join us," Paige called.

Sarah pointed over her shoulder. "My suit's in my bag, which is in the car."

Natalie, whose back had been to her, swiveled and grinned. "Suit, schmuit. Just whip off your clothes and get your ass in here. No one's around but the staff, and the bubbles will cover your unmentionables when they come around."

"I think I need a beer—or five—first."

The aproned woman reappeared, cold bottle neatly tucked into a koozie, which she handed to Sarah. Apparently, she'd heard the exchange because she said, "Four more beers coming right up." She turned a smile on the trio of wet women and took their drink orders while Sarah tipped the bottle to her lips and drank. The cool liquid soothed her parched throat on its way down.

"Chug! Chug! Chug!" the gaggle chanted from the hot tub. So what if she felt like she was back in college? It was better than being stuck in an argument with her stubborn husband. She had some serious catching up to do here, and she was going to have fun, by God, despite said pigheaded hunk. She plopped down on the deck beside the hot tub and joined the animated conversation that, mercifully, didn't include any talk about husbands or other sore subjects.

31

By the time she threw back her third beer—which had materialized from where, she had no clue—she was feeling blissfully boneless. A bucket of iced beers, complete with a cup of lime slices, magically appeared beside her, and a tray of full cocktails flanked one side of the hot tub deck. It was like being poolside at an all-inclusive in Mexico! And it was heating up like a Mexican resort too. She pulled off her hoodie.

"Strip! Strip! Strip!" the trio of drunk women blared.

Looking around to be sure no one was sneaking up on them, she shimmied out of her shoes, socks, jeans, T-shirt, and tank. The command to strip grew raucous, punctuated by Natalie's piercing wolf whistles, so Sarah obliged, peeling off her bra and panties and swiftly slipping into the tub up to her neck in hot water while the girls cheered and fist-bumped.

Paige raised her glass. "So glad you could join us, although you might want to work on that striptease a little more. It didn't do a thing for me."

"I wasn't stripping for *you*," Sarah laughed. "And speaking of stripteases, did you know the guys have strippers joining them on their snowmobiles tomorrow?"

"Good for them!" Natalie hollered.

Lily belted out a soulful chorus of "Why Don't You Do Right?"

"Maybe we should go find a few Chippendales for ourselves." Paige's auburn eyebrows bounced.

This was followed by toasting, more drinking, and so much laughing Sarah's sides ached.

Who needs a man when I'm surrounded by the best girlfriends on the planet? Not me, that's for damn sure.

Quinn barked a laugh at whatever the hell Shanny had just said, though he wasn't sure he could even remember the joke. His mind was solidly occupied by the *discussion* that had started in his truck just before he parked and got out. Discussion? More of a discussion winding up into a full-blown familiar argument, and judging by the fire blazing in Sarah's mismatched hazel eyes, she'd been ready to take it to the mats.

Jesus fucking Christ! Why were they going over ground so old it was missing its topsoil? Not only had the subject been beaten to death, but he had also been under the impression it had been resolved—as in they were spending their own Christmas together. By themselves. He had a special gift for her—a brand-new Jeep, completely outfitted in the back to accommodate her dog, Archer—and selfish bastard that he was, he wanted to spring it on her alone, lap up her reaction without having to share it with an audience. And it wasn't just the gift. It was wanting her for himself for the few days they'd break for Christmas. Between his schedule and her structural engineering projects, the breaks didn't come that often. In fact, these next few days for Barrett's wedding was one of those rare breaks, and it was, of course, being spent with others. The hockey season was about to get a lot longer and a whole lot more grueling, and he craved alone time with his sable-haired Sarah. Needed it for his sanity.

Was it too much ask that she send some undivided attention his way and let him lavish the same on her?

Fuck me!

T.J. slapped his shoulder. "What's eating you, Hads?"

"Me? Nothing. Just thinking about whether my truck has the right hitch for whatever snowmobile trailers we're renting tomorrow." *A total lie, but it's the first thing that popped into my frickin' mind.*

Nelson shrugged. "Grims took care of everything, so whatever he set us up with will fit. Not to mention, the rides will be sweet ... and fast."

Their team captain, Dave "Grims" Grimson, was bringing his own trailer big enough for three sleds, and Quinn and Nelson had volunteered to pull the rental trailers, which would hold two apiece. As for the machines themselves, Grims was a total motorhead; no doubt whatever they found between their legs would be finely tuned and powerful.

"Nice!" Miller chortled. "Wait. Don't you guys have clauses in your contracts about staying away from shit like motorcycles, skydiving, and snowmobiles?"

Shanny flashed a grin. "Not sure. Haven't read my fine print lately. But if the team captain's doing it, it's gotta be cool for the rest of us."

"Unless he *doesn't* have that clause in his contract," Quinn added.

"How about *you* stay behind and do 'spa day' with the girls, Hads?" Shanny high-pitched on "spa day."

Everyone laughed, including Quinn, who shook his head. "No way. Way too much estrogen for this boy. Being around one woman is as much a dose of hormones as I can take."

Shit, I shared too damn much.

Three pairs of eyes turned toward him. "So hanging with your team day in and day out isn't enough of an estrogen break?" Miller asked.

"Not when my wife's pissed at me."

Definitely shared too much.

Three heads nodded, and their expressions grew solemn, as if their wives were also pissed at them. Huh. "I feel you," Miller finally said.

"Wanna talk about it?" Nelson threw out, looking as uncomfortable making the offer as Quinn felt hearing it.

"What, share my *feewings* with you bunch of losers?" He laughed, the sound a bit hollow and forced even to his own ears. "Hell no! I'd rather get hammered and forget about it."

There was an awkward throat clear, and Shanny circled back to the snowmobiles. *Thank fuck!* "You know Grims is bringing his own, right? And you can bet your sweet ass he's been tinkering with the damn thing. Probably has it rigged to run on rocket fuel, and he'll leave us all behind on the trail, eating his fucking snow."

Nelson barked a series of Tim-the-Toolman grunts.

"What, so we're racing?" Miller asked.

Shanny took up the charge. "Hell yeah, we're racing! What, did you think we were going to leisurely loop around a perimeter in some flat meadow six times like we're on a damn carousel ride and call it good?"

The boys continued yukking it up, hurling good-natured insults at one another's manhood and tossing back the beers. Quinn joined in the jabber now and then, but his heart wasn't in it. No, it was wherever the hell Sarah had gone to, but no way would he excuse himself and go looking for her. Talk about turning in his man card! Shit, these guys would laugh him right off the property. Better to freeze his nuts off and preserve his dignity. Besides, the more he drank, the less he noticed how fucking cold his nuts actually were.

Chapter 5

DAVE AND ELLIE

D ave Grimson stole a glance at his wife's small frame curled against the truck's passenger door. Ellie's eyes were closed, her long golden lashes splayed against her creamy cheeks. With every breath moving through her chest, her strawberry-blond hair rippled. God, he was a lucky bastard! The rosy mouth he knew and loved so much was parted in that soft look that usually aroused all kinds of wicked thoughts, though not so much today. Not that she wasn't sparking certain parts of him because right now was no different than any other time when he looked at her. He *always* wanted her; he worried that want sometimes bordered on obsession. But today what he wanted most from her was to talk about a subject weighing heavy on his mind and one she neatly avoided whenever a rare stretch of alone time presented itself.

He wanted a second child with her. Now.

They'd just dropped off their baby daughter and his mom at the Millers' mountain house, and he'd been looking forward to getting Ellie alone so they could talk about that next baby because, hot damn, he was primed to start on making that kid during this getaway! But Ellie had promptly fallen asleep. Taking care of Baby Kelsey, in between taking care of him and their household, took its toll. Which might have explained why Ellie avoided the subject every time he brought it up, but he needed to make her see it wasn't good to have a big spread between the kids' ages.

With their destination a mere twenty minutes away, he was running out of time to at least get the discussion in gear.

The truck ate up the gray ribbon of road, and dusted spruce trees blurred outside the windows. Just as it occurred to him to slow the hell down and take his time getting to the house they were sharing with six other couples, Ellie stirred, letting out a cute little sigh before sinking back into her seat.

"El, you asleep?"

She blinked and straightened. "Not anymore."

"Sorry. Didn't mean to say that so loud." *Except I totally did.*

Yawning, she stretched an elbow over her head. "It's okay, hon. I need to wake up for the big party anyway. How far are we from this castle I've heard so much about?"

"Uh, twenty minutes or so? Unless you want to stop along the way?"

She fastened her pretty slate-blue eyes on him. "For what?"

He shrugged nonchalantly. "To look at the scenery?"

"It's freezing outside!" she chuckled.

"Then how about a hot chocolate?"

She swiveled her head. "Where? There's nothing around here."

"I could head into town—"

"We can get hot chocolate there, I'm sure, and once you park this rig"—she jerked a thumb over her shoulder at the snowmobile trailered behind them—"we can add something with some kick to it."

"Are you suggesting we spike the hot chocolate?" Ellie hadn't touched alcohol since she'd found out she was pregnant.

Her lips tipped up in a smile. "Maybe."

He raised his eyebrows. "Are you trying to get me drunk so you can take advantage of me?" *God, please say yes!* Baby Kelsey's arrival had taken a toll on their sex life too. A *big* toll.

37

A lilting laugh escaped her. "I don't think we need alcohol for me to take advantage of you. Besides, what makes you think you'll be the only one drinking?"

"But the breastfeeding ... I thought ..."

"I'm switching her to formula."

This took him by surprise. They really *hadn't* talked lately. "Really? Why?"

"Your daughter has taken to biting when I breastfeed her."

He felt a grin grow and split his face; he couldn't help himself. "Can't blame her. I'm rather partial to it myself."

She gave him a spectacular eye-roll. "Yes, but when *you* bite, you use some finesse. She just chomps, and those four front teeth may be tiny, but they're sharp, and she does a lot of damage with them. Ouch!"

Without his permission, his eyes strayed to her chest, appreciating how full her breasts had become. Right now he especially appreciated how they strained against the fabric of her shirt, causing a little gap between her buttons that gave him a tantalizing view of satin and lace and fleshy pale swells. Suddenly, the grin on his face wasn't the only thing growing. He pulled his eyes back to the road. "So it's healthier for you, at least as far as damage control. Is it healthy for her?"

"The doctor says she's gotten all the benefit from breastfeeding she can get. Since I'll be away from her for a few days, I thought it would be a good time to wean her."

"Huh. So what happens to ... you know?"

From the corner of his eye, he could see Ellie glance down at herself. "I expect the girls will shrink back to normal size."

Damn.

She tapped his thigh. "Don't look so disappointed."

Shit! That obvious? "Who says I'm disappointed?"

"It's written all over your handsome face. Don't worry, though. I brought along a few new pieces of sexy lingerie to help you get over it."

He patted himself on the back for not blurting what was on the tip of his tongue: "They're not deflating in a day, so let's skip the lingerie and get down to it." No, not when he was on the verge of having his wife rock his world several days in a row, like she used to do. His spine tingled just thinking about her riding him ... him riding her ... other things that involved skin-to-skin contact.

Squirming in his seat to adjust himself, he turned toward her and swallowed hard. "You did bring them with you, right? The new, uh, pieces? Maybe you should describe them to me." He didn't care if they were new, old, gauzy, or plain white cotton. It *all* looked good on her—or off her, piled on the floor.

"Or show you?" She unbuttoned her top button and batted her eyelashes at him.

Holy shit! His mouth swung wide. "Are you wearing them *now*?"

Tapping her chin thoughtfully, she said, "Hmm ... now that's a question you'll have to answer for yourself."

"As soon as we get to where we're going, I'm going to get to work on solving that mystery. Fair warning, though. Whatever sexy pieces you're hiding might not stay on for long."

"That is kind of the point of lingerie, isn't it?" She dropped her hand on his thigh and brushed her fingertips along his quad muscle, up and down, over and over.

Fuck, yeah! This getaway was more promising by the minute. Now if he could get her to move her hand a little higher ... "You keep that up, and I *will* pull over. But not to look at the scenery or search for a hot chocolate hut in the wilderness." He let out a low growl.

She rewarded him with a giggle, then canted her head toward the passenger-side window. "You did remember the condoms, right?"

Right. The dreaded condoms. It had been their only form of birth control before Ellie got pregnant, and they hadn't been religious about using them. Since Kelsey had been born, they'd shifted from an active sex life before and during the pregnancy to a sporadic one that hadn't required regular birth control; rubbers had remained their go-to. But where Ellie might have

39

been laid-back about their use *before* getting pregnant, she was militant about it now—a veritable condom Nazi. Which was one more solid check mark in the "pro" column for child number two.

He cleared his throat. "So, El, about the condoms. I've been thinking."

Her hand slid from this thigh. In his peripheral vision, she stiffened, refastened that damn button, then began scrolling through her phone.

"What are you doing?"

"I'm assuming the answer is, 'No, Ellie, I did not pack any condoms,' so I'm looking for a convenience store where we can pick some up, but I don't have any service." She thunked her forehead against the window.

"Hang on, El. I have an idea."

She swung her head toward him, and he felt the weight of her narrowed-eye glare. "Dave Grimson, I know what you're up to. If you think you're going to hoodwink me into getting pregnant with that second baby over the next few days, you are sadly mistaken. No condoms, no sex."

Fuck! Here he'd been letting his libido gallop ahead of him, imagining making love to his wife, then making it some more—without a latex barrier between them. Getting her pregnant with the next one had been his plan for the next three nights, and though he'd envisioned lots and lots of lovemaking to make that happen, the sex had been a side benefit. A *big* side benefit, with a shit ton of upside, but not the main attraction.

"No sex of *any* kind?" he squawked, trying to lighten the suddenly stormy mood, though his mind was beginning to gather thunderclouds of its own.

Arms folded over her chest, she snorted and shook her head. "I can't believe you just thought you could bamboozle—"

He raised a placating hand. "Cool your jets, El. I did bring condoms." *Two.* Meaning they'd be covered for two out of three nights and absolutely no mornings or the afternoon session—or

40

two—he'd mentally penciled into the schedule. "Can't we at least talk about this without you completely shutting me down?"

Her arms cinched down a little tighter. Not a good sign. "We *have* talked about *this*, and we agreed we would wait until you're closer to retirement."

"I know what we originally said, but that's when I thought retirement was only a year or two away. Things change. With the way my play's been going lately, Herb thinks he can ink the team to another four or five years. I don't want to wait that long to have more kids, El."

She turned to him with wide eyes. "He *does*?"

A triumphant smile threatened to break out over his face, and he wrestled it back. "Yep. That's good news, huh?"

Ellie fought the urge to slump in her seat and give in to the tears that always seemed to lurk behind her eyes these days. No, this was *not* good news. Dave's agent getting an extension on his contract was good news, of course. The team was lucky to have him, and he deserved every year and every dollar. But it also meant he'd be gone half the time. Taking care of one baby was a bigger job than she'd ever imagined, and now he was lobbying for a second one. Heck, he'd been practically lobbying for a second one as he was catching their first one coming out of the birth canal!

At least he'd been there for the entire birth. Warm tingles raced along her limbs as she recalled how his beautiful hazel eyes had glazed and shimmered with tenderness and pride at the sight of red-faced Kelsey in his big palm. He was an awesome dad—when he was around—but the minute Ellie got pregnant with number two, he'd be lobbying for number three and four and ...

And oh God, they'd only just left Kelsey behind, and Ellie would have sworn a piece of her heart had been sliced off! If they had a second child, how many more pieces would she be able to spare?

Lord, she was an absolute wreck lately, her emotions spilling over into everything and coating the finer points of logic in sticky goo.

She drew in a breath and with it—she hoped—firmness mixed with enough caring that she didn't gut him. Diplomacy was a tightrope she didn't always navigate well with her man, who was far more sensitive than his growly public persona would lead anyone to believe. She shifted in her seat to face his chiseled profile. Clipped brown hair highlighted with strands of gold, strong jaw covered in a trimmed beard, and those squared-off shoulders of his set off little bursts of fire inside her that stole her breath. She needed to push aside her lust for the moment and *focus.*

"Dave, you're gone all the time," she began, "which leaves me to deal with everything on my own. I'm struggling as it is. Having another baby would double the work." She winced inwardly at the whine in her voice.

"I'm not gone all the time, El. Yeah, we have road trips, sometimes long ones, but when I'm home, I'm *home.* With you and Kelsey because that's where I *want* to be. As I recall, you practically shoved me out of the house the other day because you said I was in your way."

"No, Dave, what I said was you looked bored and I needed some groceries but was exhausted and would you please help me out by going to the store." *I knew he took that wrong. So much for diplomacy. Rack up a point for hurt feelings.*

His frustration showed in his exaggerated exhale. "I'm not gone that much," he grumbled.

Yes, you are!

It struck her that whenever Dave was home, her world tilted back to even keel. Having him around soothed something deep in her soul, and it wasn't merely because he pitched in a lot, especially with the baby. He was her rock, her strong oak tree to lean on, her world.

Did he have to be present to be all those things she needed? And why did she need them so badly? Maybe she'd turned into a big wuss. Other wives managed the load just fine. Though Ellie had sold off her business and did very little landscape design these days, running their household was ... overwhelming. What was wrong with her? Where had that independent businesswoman gone? She was reliant—too reliant—on this man she adored. How long before he tired of the blubbering, clinging mess she'd become? She was a shell of the woman he'd fallen in love with. Capable Ellie Hendricks had disappeared, body-snatched by Ellie Grimson.

Okay, knock it off. You're being overly dramatic again.

Her mind roamed to when he was gone. The loneliness was positively paralyzing.

And then came the tears, welling in her eyes once more. How could she be a good mom to *one* child when emotions clouded everything?

It came as no surprise he wanted more kids. He'd always been clear about that, and she'd been right there with him. But now, to divide up what few reserves she had between two—

The nav system jolted her from her dark thoughts when it announced a turn up ahead. Dave took it, and they rode along in stilted silence. Ellie absorbed the manicured landscape, lovely despite its dormant state, getting lost in the vista that unfolded around them. Eventually it opened onto a sprawling stone-and-timber ... castle.

"Looks like we have a welcoming committee," Dave said in his deep baritone.

Standing in front of the mansion stood four men she couldn't quite make out. "You recognize them?"

"Yep." He slowed the truck and gave her a sidelong glance full of flint. "Look, El, I don't know exactly what I said to land me in the I-Have-No-Fucking-Clue-What-I-Just-Did-Wrong zone, but don't freeze me out, huh?"

Her mouth dropped open. She snapped it shut as fire flared in her tummy. "That's not fair! I was looking at the landscaping; I

43

wasn't freezing you out! Why does it have to be your way or the highway? And you know *exactly* what you said, so don't act like this is all me, Dave."

Ellie Hendricks was back, and she was spewing flames. Why did it take anger to wake the girl up?

He nosed the truck toward the edge of a parking area, slammed it into park, and turned off the engine. "Right," was all he said. His eyes flicked toward the windshield. "Here they come. Let's pretend we're having a great time." His mouth pulled into a brittle smile that resembled a grimace.

She trilled a sarcastic laugh. "Sure, Captain. Whatever you say." Flinging her door open, she planted her boots firmly on the ground and banged it shut with all she was worth. From the corner of her eye, Dave flinched as he heaved himself out of the truck. *Good!* She turned and spread her arms wide to hug T.J., who was coming toward her with a cockeyed smile. Matching that smile, she amped up the brilliance for good measure.

"Hey, El," he said as he wrapped her up in a quick hug. "The girls are inside."

The other guys lined up for their hugs, but their eyes roved over the covered sled trailered behind the truck. When they were done hugging on her and saying hello, they drifted toward a grinning Dave. Of course *that* smile he sported was genuine. As she hauled her bag out of the truck, he hauled off the tarp protecting the snowmobile, seemingly oblivious to her presence. A round of "holy shits," man gasps, and laughter rippled through the air. Making her way to the front entry, Ellie left them all behind, sure she was out of Dave's mind before she'd gotten out of his sight.

Chapter 6

MAC AND MIA

*M*ia Morales clapped excitedly in the passenger seat and would have bounced but for the seat belt restraining her. "This is going to be so much fun!" She and her fiancé, Dana "Mac" McPherson were wending their way leisurely along I-70 toward the party mansion her boss, Paige Miller, had rented for the next three days. Well, technically Mac's teammate Blake had rented it, but Paige had helped him find it. And Mia had drooled over the pictures alongside Paige as they clicked through the gallery on Paige's computer, and she couldn't wait to spend time exploring the property.

Behind the wheel, Mac ran a hand through his wavy brown hair and nodded his agreement. "Yeah, it'll be nice to spend a few days away from the kids."

Her parents had taken Mac's son and daughter to a different party house—the Millers' mountain home—which was likely a cross between a circus and the inside of jumping castle by now, filled with adults and kids of all ages and sizes shrieking at the tops of their lungs. The kids, not the adults. Although ...

Mia snuggled against Mac's arm. "I've never been to a mountain wedding in the winter. It's going to be so *romantic*."

"Romantic until we freeze our asses off," he chuckled. "You looking for some romance there, Loops?"

"Not if you're going to use my old nickname."

"From this moment forward, no childhood nicknames that invoke sweet, colorful cereal shall pass these lips," he declared. "And speaking of lips, give me a kiss."

Obliging, she craned her head, and he turned his to steal a kiss before returning his focus to the road.

She settled against him with a sigh. "Sounds like you're looking to catch a little romance yourself, Mr. Goalie. So we're on the same page."

"Most definitely. Which leads me to ... I think we should talk about setting the date for our own wedding."

The warm bubbles that had been fizzing in her bloodstream suddenly popped. She straightened and frowned. "Can't it wait?"

Mac slid her a sidelong glance, his big blues sparkling, and sighed. "Mia, it's *been* waiting for months. Sweetheart, I want to set a date that's not five years from now. I'm ready to get on with building that life with you, *our* life as a family, starting now. The kids—"

"I know, I know." Her cheeks blazed, with what, she wasn't sure. Not quite anger, not quite guilt, not quite fear, though perhaps a mix of all three. Officially, they were engaged, but there was a "no expiration date" on the commitment rather than a tangible plan to close the deal. And she was the holdout. Mac hadn't been bashful about declaring his readiness to tie the knot, nor had his kids. Everyone was ready ... except her.

Folding her arms across her chest, she stared out the window at the dark pines soaring above white snowfields and craggy rock. His big, warm hand landed on her thigh and squeezed. "I want us to live under the same roof. I want to wake up with you next to me in bed. I want us to strike up our hillbilly band on a whim because we're all together and it just happens, not because we planned it. I want to come downstairs to you and Riley flipping pancakes." His voice was low, gentle, but somehow she still ground her back molars. "I don't understand why you constantly avoid the subject, Mia. Are you having second thoughts about marrying me?"

"No." The word came out like a whip snapping between her clenched teeth.

He withdrew his hand, gripped the wheel with it, and pushed a breath through his nose. The temperature in his Mercedes SUV seemed to drop below the twenty degrees icing the world outside their enclosed cab.

Regret had her backpedaling. "I'm sorry, Mac, it's just ... I'm just ... It's a lot ..."

Her thoughts scattered to the wind, and as she tried to line them up in some semblance of order, she tilted her head to look at him, cringing at what she saw. His square jaw might have been dotted with stubble, but it wasn't so thick it hid the bunched muscle flexing there. He canted his head toward her, his brows low and tight across eyes that had transformed from clear sapphire to churning-ocean blue. "Why won't you just come clean with me? If you don't want to get married, just say it!"

"And then what?" she blurted.

Eyes forward again, he pushed a huge breath through his chest. At least he was getting in his deep breathing exercises. "And then we figure out if this is really going to work."

Holy Javier! "Why can't we just go along at the pace we've been going?" she squeaked.

One corner of his mouth twisted with an ironic curl. He shook his head, those silken strands she loved to weave her fingers through brushing his neck. "Seriously, Mia? How many times have we had this same discussion now? That is, when I can even pin you down long enough to *have* the discussion."

"You can pin me down anytime you want, big boy." She batted her lashes at him. The tic in his jaw pulsed more vigorously, and breath caught in her throat. "Does this mean you're not interested in pinning me down?" The humor she was going for came out stilted.

His fingers tightened their stranglehold on the steering wheel. "This isn't funny. Not to me."

"But I—"

47

"I need you to not evade the question for a change," he growled. "Something's stopping you, and shit if I can figure out what it is. *You* certainly aren't telling me." He whipped his head toward her again, the look on his face the very one he used to face down opponents crashing into his net. *Whoa!* "Is it the kids? You don't want to be a mom? Or is it me?" And there went his head again, swiveling back to the front.

"It's none of those!" she protested to his stony profile. "I want to marry you, Mac. I want to be a real mom to your kids. I do." Her voice sounded reedy, as if she were trying to overcome a lie.

She loved this man with all her heart. She loved his kids too and could not imagine being apart from him or them. Ever. So why wasn't she jumping in with both feet?

"I'm not sure I believe you anymore, Mia." The navigation system blared that they needed to turn off the highway.

Once they wound their way along the private drive for a few hundred yards, she choked out, "What now?"

"I don't know." His voice was soft, heartbreakingly resigned. "Things have been really intense. I don't know how much more I can take. Maybe we need to step back."

She stifled a gasp. "What do you mean, 'step back'?"

Looking around as if checking out their surroundings, he was quiet for long, breathless moments.

"Mac?" she prodded.

He lifted his chin at the windshield. "Looks like we're here."

"What did you mean by 'step back'?" she repeated in a suffocated whisper. A cluster of guys came into view, and they all looked up and signaled greetings from where they stood, surrounding a gleaming snowmobile on the back of a trailer.

Mac eased the Mercedes beside Quinn's black truck and cut the engine. His big blues fastened on her face. "Just what I said. Maybe we need some time off, time away from each other so we can think clearly and figure out what it is we both want." Nowhere on his handsome face was there a flicker of humor. The man was dead serious, and a rush of panic ignited in her chest, constricting her throat. Stinging tears welled behind her eyes.

She opened her mouth, to say what, she wasn't sure, but before any words could tumble out, he stepped from the SUV and called a hello to the guys. Before he joined them, he leaned in. "Looks like the girls are somewhere else, so why don't you go find them? I'll get our bags later, after I figure out where everyone's sleeping." He paused a beat. "Maybe they have an extra room I can hole up in."

The dam burst, filling her eyes. "You mean you want to take a break *now*? Today?" Her voice straddled a line between shrill and strangled.

His tone, however, deepened, taking on an unsettling, detached quality. "Better to figure these things out now, don't you think?"

Before she could tell him no, she didn't agree, he had pivoted and closed his door. She watched his broad, retreating back while her heavy heart sank to her knees.

Fuck. Me! Mac wanted to yell. Instead, he mustered a semblance of a smile as he approached his buddies ogling a snowmobile. With their attention riveted on the machine, they barely looked at him, for which he was grateful. He needed a few seconds to compose himself, to wrangle the anger and anguish twining inside him. Stuffing his hands into the front pockets of his jeans, he rocked on the balls of his feet, and tried—but failed—not to steal a glance at Mia over his shoulder.

Her back was to him, her long dark hair swaying in cadence with her leggings-encased ass peeking out from a dark puffy jacket. He didn't need to see her face. The expression she'd worn when he'd ducked his head inside the car was indelibly etched in his mind: delicate sable brows arched above wide espresso eyes shimmering with tears, high cheekbones brushstroked in vivid pink, full, parted lips in a matching hue. The sum total of her parts was stupefaction that he would suggest such a thing as taking time off from their relationship. At least she hadn't cheered the idea, so there was that.

Had he really meant it? He wasn't sure. He didn't want to lose her, but did he even really have her? The ring on her finger said so, but it was no guarantee of a future together.

What the fuck was her deal anyway? She'd agreed to marry him—hell, she'd bowled him over when she'd accepted—so why was she dragging this out? Cold feet? If that was the case, she needed to come clean. Now. It was one thing to keep him dangling on a string, but this wasn't just about him. It was about Mason and Riley, who'd grown dangerously attached to Mia. Dangerous because if she pulled the rug out from under them ... She was being unfair. The kids came first. Except so did she. He longed for that future with her, and he was anxious to get it started. Things between them had been so good, and he only imagined them getting better. But if they didn't work out ... No, he wasn't going there. He could search the rest of his life and he'd never find anyone he loved the way he loved her. This he knew to the depths of his soul.

Did he want her *too* much? Was he *too* anxious to start their life together? Was he pressuring her too much? Shit, no! He'd been giving her tons of space, and now it was time to claim happiness for the kids and for himself. Time to grow a pair and stand up for what he wanted, for what the kids deserved. No more Mr. Patient Guy.

He laughed because the guys were laughing. At what, he had no fucking clue. Didn't matter. At least he was in a safe haven among his bros. *Must turn off brain.* When someone shoved a beer at him, he didn't hesitate to tip the bottle back and down half of it in one go.

"Whoa! Someone's thirsty," Nelson chuckled.

"Long drive," he croaked before finishing it off. "Got anything stronger?"

A murmur of agreement ran through the guys, and when Hadley suggested they step inside and throw back a shot or two,

Shanstrom mumbled something about staying out of the girls' way.

Grimson carefully stretched a tarp over his sled, like he was tucking a baby into its crib. "I'm down with that. Doesn't this place have wings so we can stay on our side and they can stay on theirs?"

Huh. Interesting. At least the boys were all on the same page ... or the same side of the building, at any rate.

Miller nodded. "Sure does. How about we head to the game room? We can play pool or poker or air hockey. They even have a few old-time arcade games."

"Any booze?" Mac asked.

Miller's eyebrows bounced. "Fully stocked bar, baby."

"A nice comfy couch, and I've just found my home away from home for the next few days," Shanstrom chortled.

The group of six slunk into the house, following Miller, who headed away from a distant chorus of giggling drifting from another part of the house. Mac was so intent on dumping his dismal thoughts from his brain that he didn't pay attention to his surroundings as they went, though he had the vague impression of being in a European hotel or a castle.

"This place come with a map?"

"Don't need one," Miller replied. "We'll find everything we need in this section. Hell, we can hole up for days. Weeks even."

Mac released a relieved breath. Not that he had any desire to hole up for days, but finding a room to himself would be a piece of cake. No one would even notice him keeping his distance from Mia.

Chapter 7

BLAKE AND MICHAELA

Michaela Wagner plowed her fingers through her curls, cleared her throat, and wiggled in the passenger seat. For the third time in the past half hour. Sat as far forward as the seat belt would allow and smacked her palms against her jean-covered knees.

Beside her, sprawled behind the steering wheel, looking as relaxed as a koala high on eucalyptus leaves—a very *large* koala—sat the man who would be her husband in two days. *Husband! Two days!* The thought both made her blood effervesce with happy champagne bubbles and terrified the crap out of her at the same time.

Said koala reached out and tugged a curl. "If I didn't know better, I'd say you're fidgety over there, gorgeous. What's going on?"

She swiveled her head to look at him, and her heart fluttered. *Speaking of gorgeous!* Short blond hair, twinkling green eyes, clean-shaven jawline as sculpted as the rest of his body, and a full mouth that was presently curved in an adorable smirk. She loved it all, loved looking at every perfect feature, couldn't get her fill of Blake Barrett. *Her* Blake. Would she ever? *Nope.* "Aren't you just the least bit nervous?"

"About what?"

"Oh, I don't know." She clapped her palm against her forehead dramatically. "No, wait! I think I got this! I do know! About getting married!" A laugh escaped, taking a tiny measure of anxiety with it.

He swung his head toward her and pinned her with those fern-green eyes of his for an instant. Amusement, adoration, and tenderness converged and danced there, stealing the breath from her lungs.

Shaking his head, he turned his focus forward. "No. Why would I be?"

"Because it's forever."

"And your point is?"

"It's ... permanent."

"M, don't tell me you're getting cold toes."

"Feet."

"Those too?" he chuckled.

"I'm not getting cold feet. I'm just ... nervous ... excited ... all kinds of other emotions I can't put words to. Mostly excited."

He pried one of her hands apart from the other one and lifted it to his lips, planting a soft kiss on a knuckle. Then he laced his fingers with hers and cradled their joined hands on his thigh. The feel of his strong hand and the press against solid muscle uncoiled some of the kinks in her stomach, and she pulled in a steadying breath.

"Are you nervous about spending the rest of your life with me?" he asked softly.

She didn't hesitate. "No, never. That feels right. *So* right. Maybe I'm nervous about flubbing my lines."

"Okay, now *that* part makes me nervous too. But we don't have that many lines to flub, and the minister is going to prompt us."

"How about we rush through the ceremony and get to the kiss?"

"Seal the deal? Now you're talking!"

She leaned across the console and rested her head on his shoulder, warmth oozing through her at the thought they were in this *together*. Forever.

With her free hand, she hugged his bicep, and he gave her a little flex, making her giggle. "Ooh, such muscles you have, Mr. Bear."

"You just wait. After we ditch our guests tonight, I'll show you my *special* muscle."

She straightened with a grin. "Actually, it's an organ. And it's not coming out to play tonight."

"What, my right pec? That's the muscle I was talking about." Executing a flex of his chest this time, he made the fabric of his long-sleeved tee jump. His mouth curled lazily into a cocky smirk. "What muscle were *you* thinking of? And why isn't it allowed to come out and play tonight?"

"Because it's right before our wedding, so we're sleeping in separate rooms."

His eyes went wide. "Wait. What? I didn't get that memo."

"It's tradition, like the groom not being allowed to see the bride before the ceremony on their wedding day. No sex until we're officially married."

"I'm not sure I want to go through with this wedding now. I had big plans for that hot little body of yours tonight."

She gave his shoulder a playful shove. "You'll have to save those plans for a few days. Besides"—she whispered as she gave his ear a flick of her tongue—"you're going to need all your strength for our wedding night."

He let out a guffaw. "You know how much I love a challenge. You'd better be ready."

"Oh, I will be." She wiggled her eyebrows at him, then turned to look out the window. "I think this is the entrance to our place coming up."

His gaze darted to the nav screen on the dashboard. "Looks like." He took the turn, then coasted to a stop and put the Range Rover in park.

"What are you doing?"

He crooked his finger at her. "Come here, and you'll find out."

She leaned in with a smirk of her own, and he pulled her to him for a long, tender, breath-stealing kiss.

"What was that for?" she gasped when he released her.

A mist glossed his eyes, and he stroked her cheek with his finger. "I just want you to know I love you with all my heart, and I can't wait to start this new adventure with you."

Unexpected tears surged, filling her eyes, wedging a lump in her throat. She swallowed hard, trying to regain her voice, but it came out in a choke. "I love you too, Blake. With my heart, body, and soul."

Paralyzed, Blake stared into M's silver pools, a wave of emotion crashing over him, sweeping him into their depths. He saw his future reflected there, saw only her, and his heart swelled to near bursting. *I get to look at those eyes for the rest of my life.* Several beats passed before he got his throat working again, and he gulped in a breath. "I'm one hell of a lucky guy," he croaked.

She nodded, her silky sable curls bouncing. "So am I."

He corkscrewed a curl around his finger and forced a grin. "Except you're not a guy, and thank God for that."

His phone chimed with a text, and he untangled his finger from her hair to pick it up.

"You're frowning," she said. "Everything okay?"

"Yeah. It's just Fergs saying he'll be running a little late but that he'll still make it here before the wedding." Owen Ferguson, Blake's best friend since childhood and his best man, was now playing in the AHL and had a game the next night. Consequently, he couldn't make it for anything but the wedding itself.

"I should hope so," she scoffed. "Is Tracy coming with him?"

"Don't know. I'm not sure if they're together this week or broken up again. Does it make me a dick that I've stopped keeping track?"

"No, it makes you practical. Trying to stay up on that relationship would make anyone's head spin."

"Agreed. And honestly, the only relationship I give two shits about is this one." He flicked a finger between them.

"Well, as long as it's *two* shits and not just one ..." She laughed and dropped a full-lipped kiss on his mouth. "We should probably get going. Nothing screams bad manners like the guests of honor showing up a couple of hours late."

"You sure sex is off the table tonight?" His dejected tone was mostly a joke, though he was already missing her weight against him. She was a snuggler, and he'd grown used to drifting off to sleep with her soft curves pressed against him. That, more than their indescribable lovemaking, was what he missed most when he was on the road, and it wasn't a habit he cared to relinquish when she was nearby.

She gave him a mischievous smile. "Sorry, but it's not on the table, the bed, or anywhere else. You'll have to be patient. Think you can keep your hands off me for a few days?"

"No." Putting the Range Rover into gear, he nosed it back on the road and slid her a side-eye. "I take it no heavy petting either?"

"Who says 'heavy petting'?" Her grin broadened. "Apparently, you. It sounds like you're discussing a dog or a cat."

"Did you know that cats have been domesticated only half as long as dogs?"

"I did not know that," she chuckled. That chuckle transformed into a gasp when they rounded a curve and a stone castle came into view. "Oh. My. God. I wasn't expecting ... I mean, I saw the pictures, but this ... Oh. My. God."

Blake let out a low whistle as he took in the colossal structure. It reminded him of the Redstone Castle, a twenty-million-dollar spread he and his teammates had joked about buying and converting into their own personal version of Disneyland, Colorado style. "Nice place. I think it'll do."

M's eyes and gaping mouth remained frozen as he wound his way up the drive, and they were still that way when he parked among his teammates' cars and killed the engine. He gently lifted her chin; she startled back to the present and closed her mouth. "Wow," she whispered reverently.

Pride surged inside him. He had spent hours with Paige Miller searching for the perfect venue, and this place had been his top pick. Paige had wheeled and dealed with the owner, but it had still cost a small fortune. Seeing the look on M's face was worth every penny spent.

He grabbed their bags and they headed inside, where they were greeted by a pleasant woman dressed in black from head to toe, the only color a red apron tied at her waist. "You must be the bridal couple. We've been expecting you. If you'll come this way, I'll show you your suites and you can drop off your bags." They followed her up a sweeping staircase that brought to mind Rhett Butler carrying a kicking Scarlett O'Hara up to bed in *Gone with the Wind*. Maybe later he could carry M up the staircase, minus the kicking.

The woman paused and opened a door, interrupting his musings. "This is your room ... until the wedding night." A twinkle lit her eyes as she motioned for Blake to step inside and deposit his stuff. He'd scarcely swept his gaze around the spacious dark-paneled bedroom before falling in line behind the woman, who led them through a series of hallways to, it turned out, the opposite side of the castle. A hell of a long, confusing walk if he was going to find his way to M in the middle of the night. *Should have left bread crumbs.*

"The master suite is right through here." She motioned to a vestibule with a set of tall paneled double doors, which she pushed open.

M's gasp shot another bead of pride straight to his already puffed-up chest. She twirled in the center of a living room that oozed luxury, coming to a stop in front of a massive marble fireplace bright with flames.

"I'll leave you two alone. Just so you know, the women are presently hot-tubbing, and the men are in the game room."

M came to a stop and blinked. So did Blake. "And how do we find them? Do you have a map to this place?" he quipped.

She offered to guide them, and he stowed M's suitcase and garment bag in a closet the size of the team's training room. Down another series of hallways and stairs they went until the woman led them out of the building to a large enclosed pavilion booming with old-time crooner music and raucous female shrieks.

M paused outside the door, cupping the side of her mouth. "Sounds like the party already started."

Their guide grinned. "Yes, the ladies have been enjoying themselves." She tilted her head at Blake. "Perhaps you'd care to follow me to the game room now?"

M grabbed his hand and dragged him with her. "At least say hello to everyone before you run off to play with the boys."

"Uh ..."

The woman seemed to be warning him about something, but her voice was drowned out when he and M stepped inside and the shrieks amplified, ringing his ears as they ricocheted around the pavilion's wooden walls.

"The happy couple is here!" screeched Paige, holding up a tumbler of brown liquid as she wobbled to her feet—and promptly lost her balance, dropping back into the tub with a splash. Her head went under, but she held the glass aloft, and when she surfaced, she was laughing so hard she could barely catch her breath.

Lily, who seemed to be in the same drunken state, reached out a steadying arm. "Y-you okay?" she laughed.

"I'm fantastic!" Paige sang.

Natalie bounced up from the bubbles. "Hi, Bear!"

"Get in the water, Micky Wags!" shouted Ellie. "You can join us too, Blake."

A series of giggles erupted.

M shot him a wary glance before addressing her girlfriends with a jerk of her thumb over her shoulder. "I need to get my suit—"

"No, you don't!" Mia began to rise, then promptly slipped back beneath the water up to her neck, but not before Blake caught a glimpse of wet skin. Lots of it. "Whoops!" she giggled loudly.

It was then Blake realized three things: A familiar tune he couldn't place was blaring, the huge-ass hot tub was on full froth mode, and some of the women were completely nude.

Shit! He darted his eyes to the ceiling, desperate to escape, not wanting to have *that* conversation with any of his buddies. *Yeah, I saw your wife naked. Please don't kill me.*

"Oh shit, I think we broke Blake!" Sarah guffawed. "It's okay to look. We're under cover, so to speak."

He looked—very quickly, to be polite—before craning his head as though looking for the source of the music. He cleared his throat, his T-shirt collar suddenly too snug. "Uh, who sings this?"

Lily, who wore a one-piece—*thank fuck!*—propped an elbow on the rim of the tub. "Harry Connick, Junior. It's 'A Wink and a Smile' from *Sleepless in Seattle*." She started singing along.

"Ooh, I just *love* that movie!" exclaimed Ellie.

"So do I!" Paige concurred. "Isn't Tom Hanks so adorable in that?"

Natalie bobbed her head. "Kind of like Mac, with that whole irresistible widowed dad thing going on."

"Except I'd rather have Tom Hanks," Mia groused.

Double shit. He needed to get out of here. He dashed helpless eyes to M, who tilted her head toward the door. Amusement tugged her lips. "You've paid your dues. Why don't you go find the guys?"

"No, Blake should come swim with us!" cried Ellie. He dared a look, and heat blazed up his neck and over his face; he about had a heart attack. The big bad Grim Reaper's wife was *also* naked, and she wasn't exactly hiding it.

Fuck.

Fuck, fuck, fuck.

He didn't want his face rearranged, especially not before the wedding.

"I'll just—"

M nodded, mouthing, "Good idea. Love you."

"Love you too," he tossed out as he spun and ran for the door, chased by cackles, R-rated comments, and a "No men allowed anyway!" Closing the door behind him, he distinctly heard, "Men suck," which brought an ear-splitting cheer. What the hell had he just landed in? And how the hell was he going to find his way to his brethren and safety?

The woman in black appeared and flashed him a grin. "I tried to warn you it's a little, shall we say, rowdy in there. I'll take you to your band of brothers." Soon she was walking him to a *different* side of the castle.

As they wound their way into the mansion's depths, male voices grew louder. "Don't tell me," he said dryly. "The guys started their party too."

She nodded. "Can I bring you something to drink or eat?"

"Club soda with lime would be great. Thanks."

"Hmm. If you're a drinking man, you might want something a little stronger to catch up to these boys."

He cocked an eyebrow. "That bad?"

She shrugged. "Not so different from the women."

Just then, a shout reached his ears. "Why are women so fucking sensitive about every goddamn little thing?" This was followed by clacking noises.

He exchanged a look with the woman. "It feels like I'm walking into a battle of the sexes or something."

"It does feel that way, doesn't it?" She indicated a heavy oak door that stood ajar, then hustled away.

Pushing the door open, he strolled into a gigantic game room, where his buddies surrounded a pool table. They shouted his name and greeted him one by one with bro hugs and back slaps.

"Glad you could make it," Nelson grunted.

"How are the nerves holding up?" Grims laid a meaty paw on his shoulder, and Blake cringed. *Yes, your wife was naked, but I saw zip. Then how did I know she was naked, you ask? Uh ...*

"You sure you want to go through with this?" Hadley jarred him back to the game room, a serious look etched into his normally relaxed features. *Yes, Sarah was naked too. But I didn't look. I swear.*

"Of course I do," Blake scoffed.

"Your funeral," Mac grumped.

Something told Blake Mac's comment had nothing to do with Mia being naked, though it might have something to do with Mia preferring Tom Hanks over him.

What the hell was wrong with everyone anyway? Before he got a chance to ask, T.J. held up a half-empty whiskey bottle. "Okay boys, break time's over. Let's get back to getting utterly shit-faced." He pointed at Blake. "As the groom, you don't get a pass. And trust me, you're going to *want* to be liquored up."

"Unconscious is more like it," chimed Miller, leaning so heavily on his pool cue that he snapped it in half and stumbled sideways. The guys whooped and clapped.

Jesus, Blake was in for a rough night.

He stumbled along the hallway, unsure if he was headed the right way. The paintings on the walls looked familiar. Then again, so did the paintings in every other hallway in this damn castle maze.

He reached the vestibule with the double doors and straightened, running a hand over his hair, his jaw. What if he had the wrong room? His eyes swept the dim surroundings. No other bedrooms in this part of the mansion, so he wasn't about to blunder into the wrong bed—which would have added more insult on the injury dealt to his psyche during the hot tub incident.

With stealth he wasn't sure he possessed, he eased one of the doors open, closing it softly behind him. Embers glowed in the marble fireplace, and he breathed a sigh of relief that he'd sneaked into the right room. He stripped off his clothes, tiptoed into the bedroom, and slid between the sheets. Moonlight streamed through a window, bathing everything in silver. The smell of chlorine wafted from the covers, and an image of M naked in the hot tub bolted to his dick, waking it up.

No sex. But that didn't mean no snuggling.

Dressed in a cami and panties, she moaned and rolled to her side, presenting her back, which he pulled to his front as he encircled her in his arms. He kissed her cheek, pushed her curls aside, and rested his head against hers on the pillow.

"Blake?" she mumbled.

"Mm-hmm."

"What time is it?"

"Almost four."

She turned her head. "Were you sleeping in your own room?"

"Nope. Just now coming to bed."

"I thought we agreed no sex."

"I never agreed, but I'm not here for sex. I'm here to cuddle my girl until I have to get up in three hours."

She settled her head back on the pillow with a sigh and covered his arms with hers. "Aw, that's sweet." After a beat, she said, "If you're not here for sex, then what's that club doing poking me in the butt?"

"That *club* is in its natural state when it's next to you," he murmured. "Just ignore it. It'll go away."

"Are you drunk?"

"Think so. Are you?"

"Don't know. I went to bed two hours ago, and I'm not sure if that was enough time to sleep off any alcohol. Sounds like the guys outdid the girls tonight."

"Mm-hmm. And they're still at it. At least I left a couple of them duking it out in an air-hockey-a-thon. The rest are passed out on the couches in the game room. Except Miller, who's snoring on the floor."

She turned in his arms, facing him, and blinked. "They're sleeping in the game room?"

"If they're sleeping, yeah."

"You guys hung out in the game room all night? Except for that weird dinner we had?"

The "weird" dinner had been a gourmet buffet laid out by some famous chef Paige had hired. The guy had to have felt have let down because the girls had wandered into one family room to eat and watch a chick flick, and the guys had taken over a different family room while they ate and watched *John Wick*. Only he and M had shared the meal, and they'd sat at the kitchen counter and praised the hell out of the food, hoping to slick down any ruffled chef feathers.

"No. We spent a few hours jumping from snowbanks into a hot tub and back again."

"In your trunks?"

He nodded. "In our trunks."

"Sounds cold."

"It's a guy thing. Lots of bravado and few brain cells, with alcohol being a contributing factor."

She hummed her agreement. "So I heard a rumor about another guy thing."

"What's that?"

"You're taking strippers on your snowmobiles tomorrow."

He barked a laugh, and her eyes startled wide. "You're kidding, right?"

She shrugged. "The girls are convinced it's a possibility."

"So what's the scenario? We plop naked girls in front of us on our sleds and take them into the woods, where we race around for a few hours and hope they don't freeze to death? Or maybe they use saplings for poles and dance in platform heels and G-strings in the snow until they turn into Smurfs?"

"Smurfs?"

"Blue skin." To his relief, she snickered. "Jesus, M, we'll have enough to do just racing the damn snowmobiles. I've been looking forward to this. I want to open it up and fly. I can't do that with *anyone* along for the ride. Besides, I told the guys no titty show. Well, unless you're the one giving the titty show, and then it's in a private room for my eyes only."

Her shoulders shook with laughter. "Okay. I have to admit I was a little skeptical of the logistics." Her voice dropped, low and sweet. "So are you the only one who came to bed?"

"Mm-hmm." He stroked the curls off her face. "I have a feeling the other guys aren't welcome in their beds."

She traced figure eights on his chest with her fingertip, sending shivers to his scalp. "Tonight was not what I expected. Why do you think everybody's so mad at everybody else?"

He shifted so he could see her better. "No idea. The guys decided talking about women was off-limits tonight, so we stuck to sports and things with wheels. How about the girls? Did they talk about what was going on?"

"No. The only men they talked about were actors and Chef Justin."

He laughed. "The chef?"

"Why are you looking at me like that? He's a great cook, and he's kinda cute." She pressed herself closer. "The, um, club isn't going away. If anything, it's gotten *harder* to ignore." A low, throaty laugh rolled through her, making the appendage in question more wood-like.

He nuzzled her nose with his. "Maybe you should stop looking all hot and sexy, though I'm not sure that's possible."

"Charmer."

He heard the smile in her voice, and it emboldened him. "You know, this cuddling thing would work a lot better if we didn't have your clothes between us." He dropped his mouth to the base of her neck and softly sucked a trail to a tender spot below her ear. She rewarded him by dropping her head back on a moan, and hope climbed inside him. He continued working his way along her neck, her jaw, to her ear, where he nibbled and teased with his tongue. Snaking his hands beneath the waistband of her tiny panties, he stroked her smooth ass. "This isn't sex," he murmured.

"No?" she breathed, rocking against him. "That's too bad."

His cock jumped, and he pulled back. "Are you considering bending your pre-wedding rule?"

"Not exactly," she murmured, delighting him when she pulled off her cami. "That rule applied to last night and tonight." She took his hands in hers and placed them on her full breasts. He palmed them eagerly, and she arched her back into his touch. A beat later, she wriggled out of her panties and glided against him, all warm silky skin. "I never said anything about morning."

Whatever problems had gripped the other couples flew from his mind as he rolled his soon-to-be-wife on her back and, in the moon's glow, showed her how much he loved her over and over.

Chapter 8

THE HIGH MARK

hree hours later, despite barely an hour of sleep and
eyes that felt like they were filled with sand, Blake
couldn't stop grinning as his gaze roved over his
disheveled buddies. He probably looked as bad as they did, but
he didn't care because he had the best reason for lack of sleep.
He'd made love to M languidly and thoroughly, a slow burn that
had pulled four orgasms from her before igniting into a full-on
conflagration for them both. "No sex" had turned out pretty
damn well. When he'd abandoned her bed a short while ago,
he'd proudly left her sated and sleeping.

He clapped his hands and rubbed his palms together, causing
a few of his semiconscious friends to flinch. "We ready to start
this bachelor party?"

"Fuck you, Barrett," Hadley groaned.

"I'm the groom," Blake protested.

"Would you wipe that fucking grin off your fucking face?"
groused Shanstrom. "I don't give a fuck if you're the groom. It's
fucking obscene."

Blake's grin broadened. "Well, good morning to you too,
sunshine." He mentally did a head count. "Hey, where's Mac?"

"I think he's still passed out on the game room floor," Miller
grumbled.

"Dumb fuck," Grims griped. "Nelson, go get him."

Nelson slid his sunglasses down his nose, revealing dark pouches below his eyes the color of a rhubarb stalk. "You talking to me?"

"No, I'm talking to your wife," Grims replied, sarcasm frosting his voice.

"At least one of us is," Nelson muttered as he headed toward the wing that housed the game room.

They were gathered in the enormous foyer, weighted down with snowmobiling gear and coolers holding their lunch, and the women were nowhere in sight—or sound. Probably sleeping in before the massages and facials and whatever the hell women indulged in during "spa day." As Blake's mind churned through waking M up later—a minute past midnight qualified as morning, right?—Mac loomed in Nelson's wake, rubbing his eyes and yawning.

"Found him," Nelson announced dryly.

"No shit, Sherlock." Grims turned on his heel, barking, "Let's go have some goddamn fun, goddamn it!"

They piled into Grims's and Hadley's trucks and Nelson's Range Rover and drove a half hour to a snowmobile rental place in the middle of seemingly nowhere. They all ducked inside and signed stacks of paperwork and got fitted with helmets—except Grims, who had brought his own. Grims trotted out of the building to supervise loading two rental sleds onto his trailer. Minutes later, when Blake and the others emerged, Grims directed Nelson, Hadley, and several rental guys in securing two trailers holding the other four snowmobiles behind Nelson's and Hadley's vehicles. Blake smirked to himself at Grims's inability to stand back and watch. Being in charge apparently was in the guy's DNA.

After being smothered in the grumpy gray clouds hovering over the other guys, Blake's cheerfulness resurfaced at the sight of the gleaming machines. His heart rate accelerated. *Yes!* He'd been wanting to snowmobile since he was a kid, but hockey or lack of opportunity or obligations always seemed to get in the way. And while he'd been ready to buy his own, Grims had suggested he and the other guys rent first to find out if the sport held appeal.

Blake didn't have to find out. He already knew it was going to land on his list of top ten things he loved—maybe even in fourth place, behind M and hockey and eating.

He and his buddies listened to instructions on operating the machines, how to get to the trailhead parking lot, and what to look for on the trails. Blake stifled an inner laugh as he recalled M's question about strippers. He'd have to share that one with the guys. Maybe it would be the thing to pull them out of their black moods.

"Let's go!" Grimson pointed at Blake. "Bear, you're with me."

Blake piled into the passenger seat of Grimson's truck, and Grims surged the vehicle out of the parking lot and onto the highway. Hadley and Nelson fell in behind, and the three vehicles formed a veritable snowmobile caravan. Blake drummed his hand on his thigh, trying to expend some of his excitement. Craning his head, he focused on the signs leading to the parking lot where they would unload their machines.

"There's the turnoff for the trailhead," Blake announced when the sign came into view. Grims blew past it.

What the hell? "The parking lot's back there." Blake looked over his shoulder. No one had turned off; the others still trailed behind.

"Nah, we're going someplace different—someplace really special for your bachelor party." A crazed look sprouted on Grims's face.

"Where?" The rental dudes had been extremely specific about going to the one trailhead and nowhere else.

Blake's phone chimed with a text from Mac. *WTF? Didn't we just pass the trailhead?*

Grims slid Blake a sidelong look. "I overheard one of the mechanics talking about a different spot where no one goes. We'll have it all to ourselves. This is going to be epic." He gunned the engine. "And if that's one of the boys asking why we didn't turn, tell him not to get his panties in a wad."

First Blake texted Mac, who was riding with Hadley, then sent Shanstrom a similar message about the change in plans. Blake shrugged off his modicum of concern over going somewhere different from where they were *supposed* to go. Grims was doing this for *him*, and that was something special.

Forty minutes later, Grimson turned off on a narrow side road and threaded his way through a corridor of towering spruce. The oppressive shadows of the massive trees pressed in on Blake, but then they emerged into a wide clearing. Beyond it lay an open meadow covered by a pristine blanket of snow inviting them to carve it up.

"This is it!" Grimson sounded positively gleeful.

Blake's qualms continued to recede, especially as the other guys spilled from their vehicles laughing and hooting.

"This is awesome!" one hollered.

Yeah, it was pretty damn spectacular.

Excitement crackled and popped as they unloaded the machines. After strapping on the coolers, they skinned on a grab bag of makeshift snowmobiling gear—Nelson was the only one besides Grimson who owned a legit snowmobile suit—and pulled on their helmets.

"Anybody got GPS on his phone?" Miller asked.

Blake held up his device. "I do."

"What do we need GPS for? Nothing's going to happen," Grims said.

Miller shrugged. "You never know. It's not like he needs to turn it on. It's just in case."

Grimson ignored the remark. "We've got full gas tanks, plenty of food, and the whole day. We don't have to turn your rides back in until four. This is going to be awesome!"

Shanstrom reached into his snow jacket and pulled out a flask he held above his head. "A little hair of the dog?"

This was greeted by Grims pulling out his own and a round of groans from the rest of the boys.

"Something to warm your insides?" Shanny persisted. Finally, he took a swallow and let out a "Whoo!" followed by, "Now that'll put hair on your chest."

Grims chuckled and took a tug off his own flask, which he passed around. Blake passed it back to Grims without taking a hit when it came to him, and the latter stowed it away and straddled his sled. "All right. Time for some fun!"

Agreement buzzed through them as they hopped aboard their rides and got situated. Blue sky overhead, sun glittering on the snow, and climbing temperature promised the perfect conditions for the day's adventure.

Pulling in a deep breath, Blake surveyed the meadow, his pulse ratcheting up. *Fresh snow, blazing speed, and a quiet forest waiting to be explored.* He couldn't wait.

They all turned on their machines, and the rumble of engines filled the clearing. Grimson took off, and they fell in behind as he led them into the meadow where they opened up their motors, gaining speed and confidence as they carved tracks in the powder and did their damnedest to one-up each other.

A half hour or so later, Grimson turned sharply and plunged into forest, following a cut between the trees. They fell in behind him once more, speeding along trails in a tangled forest. Blake felt himself being propelled through twiggy pines at mind-blowing speed. *What a rush!* Adrenalin coursed through him, and the exhilaration nearly lifted him off his seat—when he wasn't purposely rising up, trying to control the machine roaring between his legs.

They flew through the forest, raced across meadows, trying to outgun one another, and traversed the sides of mountains for what seemed a mere hour but what turned out to be several. Navigable trails had become scarcer until they had nearly disappeared, but they forged their own path. Blake had no idea where they were, but it seemed a long way from where they had started. Grimson pulled up in what resembled a three-sided, snow-filled bowl. He killed his sled and hopped off, pulling the flask from inside his suit and taking another tug before offering it up.

"Time for lunch!"

The coolers that had been strapped to several sleds came off and were plunked in the snow where they were opened to be plundered. Blake realized how starved he was, and apparently he wasn't alone because the guys attacked the food as though they hadn't eaten in a week. Lounging on their snowmobiles, they made short work of lunch and consolidated what was left into one cooler.

Miller looked around. "Where are we?"

"This, my friends," Grims said as he waved about him, "is the highlight of the day. You think what we've done so far is fun, you ain't seen fucking nothing yet. This is where the *real* fun begins." A crazy sort of gleam lit his eyes. "You are looking at one of *the* prime spots for high-marking."

Blake and a few of the guys let their confusion show.

Shanny cocked an eyebrow. "High-marking?"

Grimson pointed at one of the sloped walls towering over the bowl. "We take turns racing up and see who can reach the highest point."

Hadley glanced up, his mouth swinging open before he snapped it shut. "You're shitting me. We're racing up the fucking cliff in front of us?" Then he broke out in a maniacal grin. "That looks awesome!"

"Anyone who doesn't want to play can sit out," Grims continued. "No pressure; we won't call you out for being pussies." His smirk said otherwise, but no one appeared to want to "sit out."

Miller's grin matched Hadley's. "I'm in."

"Be a good way to blow off some steam," Shanstrom agreed.

"This is one hell of a way to do it," laughed Nelson.

"Wow," was all Mac said, but the look of joy on his face told the real story.

Blake nodded. "Pure. Adrenalin. Rush."

"Might be better than sex," Hads offered.

"Sex? What's that?" Shanstrom's sarcasm was as obvious as the slope in front of them.

"What, you too?" Mac chuffed.

"Yeah. Wasn't that you snoring next to me last night on the floor?"

"We were all frozen out last night—with maybe the exception of our groom here—but instead of grousing about it, I plan to take out my pent-up frustrations on that damn mountain." Grimson spread his arms wide. "Let's conquer this son of a bitch and see who among us can climb the highest—"

"Which will no doubt be you with that souped-up sled of yours," Miller grumped.

"Hey!" Grimson jabbed a finger in their direction and chortled. "I made sure you got the best snowmobiles. Your lead ass can't keep up? That's *your* fucking problem."

"Grims, have you high-marked this sucker before?" Nelson posed.

"Never. But when I heard the mechanic going on and on about it, I thought it'd be fun to try it out with you boys."

Shanstrom laid his head on Grims's shoulder. "Aw, I fucking love how you want to share everything with me."

Grimson gave him a shove.

"So this"—Hadley pointed upward—"is supposed to take the place of sex?"

"Not permanently, dickhead. Watch out, though. You might like it *better* than sex." Grims whacked Blake's chest and winked as he skinned on his gloves. "Let's do this!"

Animated chatter, punctuated by laughter and insults, moved through them as they pulled on their helmets and gloves.

The first one to run up the side of the mountain was Grimson, so he could show off under the guise of showing them how it was done. Next up was Miller, followed by Shanstrom. Neither man came close to Grims's mark, and they were eager to try again, heckling the others to hurry up.

As Nelson revved his motor, the guys started placing bets.

"Twenty says he won't touch either Shanny or Millsy."

"Ten says he'll beat Shanny but not Millsy."

"Anyone betting he'll top Grims?"

"Nope, I'm not taking that bet."

"Chicken."

They stood back and watched as Nelson not only beat Shanny and Miller, but nearly nudged Grimson's mark before racing back down the mountain at a speed that should have shattered the sound barrier.

"Holy shit!"

"Did you see that?"

"Oh my fucking God!"

They whooped and hollered and high-fived, and when Nelson reached the bottom and looked back up, he pumped his fist and bellowed a "Yeah!" that echoed off the mountain walls. "Not sure I'd call it better than sex," he laughed, "but what a rush! That. Was. Fucking. *Awesome!*"

"And this is only the beginning," Grims chortled. "We have plenty of time for lots more runs. I'm thinking four runs apiece—maybe five, if we push it—and we'll have our champion."

While excitement built in Blake's bloodstream, some stupid, spur-of-the moment rule about grooms going last had him cooling his jets beside his snowmobile until Hads and Mac completed their first runs. Mac flew up the mountain and edged past Grimson's mark while everyone cheered. Just as Mac turned his sled, a thudding *Whumph!* reverberated around them, followed by a rumble. Blake stared up at the mountain, his brain unable to process what his eyes were recording.

"Avalanche!" someone yelled, but Blake remained frozen in place, transfixed. Above him, the slope seemed to shift and slough its load, and Mac and his machine disappeared under a waterfall of snow.

A waterfall of white that thundered and flowed and was headed straight for them.

Realization struck that he was too late—the thing coming at them was too fast. As terror bloomed inside him, Blake began to move, registering a few of the guys running from the oncoming

73

tidal wave. Grimson, one of the few astride his sled, kicked on his engine and sped toward one side, hollering something Blake couldn't make out as impending disaster flew down the mountain and drowned out all other sound.

He ran, angling for the direction Grimson had gone, his legs churning, his body sinking, his heart pumping like a freight train as a wave of snow slammed into him. He found himself swimming on its crest, trying to keep his head up, trying not to inhale icy powder, trying not to be buried. Smothered. So many thoughts bombarded his brain, and none of them made any sense except one: *Keep your head up and keep running!* Except his legs had nothing solid to push against, no way to gain any purchase.

He felt himself get sucked under, felt himself lose the battle, felt something hard smash into his hip, and as the snow tumbled him and carried him under, his thoughts flew to a prayer that his friends would escape Mother Nature's terrible fury and that Michaela would forgive him.

Then everything spiraled into blackness.

Chapter 9

SPA DAY

*M*ichaela blinked in the bright sunlight and looked around, disoriented. Stark naked and sprawled across an unfamiliar bed, it took several moments before the delicious ache between her legs kicked in and brought back erotic memories from the night before. Well, from *hours* before because it was 11:00 a.m. and Blake had slid into her bed at 4:00 a.m.—when he'd done all kinds of wonderful things to her body until nearly six. At least she thought so. It was the timing she was hazy on, not the wonderful things. Those were very clear in her otherwise fuzz-filled brain.

A girl's got her priorities.

Rolling over, she stretched languidly, then burst into a giggle. "No sex?" she said to the room. "Yeah, right, you brazen hussy!" Poor Blake! He had been willing to keep it in the cuddle zone, but she'd seduced him, annihilating his good intentions when she'd stripped and stuffed her boobs in his hands. Not that she regretted any of it. No, sir. Knowing she had that kind of power over him was positively intoxicating, and a prideful, womanly warmth spread through her.

And if that was pre-wedding? She couldn't wait for the wedding night tomorrow! *Gotta consummate that marriage*, the lawyer in her piped up.

After a quick shower that returned her to the semblance of a human being, she made her way to the kitchen, where the scent of frying meat and cooking eggs made her mouth water and her stomach convulse simultaneously. Paige, Lily, and Ellie slumped at the island while a way-too chipper Justin flitted from cooktop to counter, chatting excitedly about his "hangover cure-all." The cooking smells assailed her, and Michaela was on the verge of hurling.

Before she could escape, though, Paige spotted her and straightened on her stool. "Mick! You survived."

"And so did you. Where's the rest of the gang?"

"They didn't survive," Lily mumbled, her head sagging in her palm.

"Not sure we did either," Ellie grumbled beside her.

Michaela plopped next to Paige and pulled her in for a side hug. "How you doing?"

"Great," Paige snorted. "As soon as my head stops pounding and my stomach descends back to its proper place."

"This will fix you right up!" Justin slid Bloody Marys under their noses. "Drink those first, then I'll serve you food and a lovely mocha espresso, light on the dairy." Paige crinkled her nose at the red concoction. "Cocktails first," he insisted in a voice that broadcast he would tolerate *no* pushback. "If you don't drink those down, you'll only throw up this meal I've created for you, and I'm not having it. Drinks and food, or nothing at all." He crossed his surprisingly beefy arms.

Paige slid Michaela uh-oh eyes and looked like she was trying not to crack up. Justin gave her an eye-roll and a finger-wag. "Ah, ah. Try it. One sip."

Paige did, and her eyes widened in surprise. "I don't even *like* tomato juice, but this is ... this is really good!"

Justin beamed at her and bowed. *What's with the bowing?* Michaela decided not to waste brain cells on the question and took a slug herself. Before long, they were tucking into an egg-scramble-spinach thing Justin had plated, and Michaela was rocking a seventy-five percent on the human scale.

"What time do we leave for our spa treatments, Paige?" Natalie rasped as she practically poured herself into the kitchen. One side of her head was a bird's nest, and the other side was flat as a pancake.

Paige checked her phone. "In a little over an hour."

"Oh, thank God!" Natalie drifted toward the coffeemaker. "I need to sweat some of this alcohol out of my pores."

Justin glowered at her.

"Uh, Nat," Paige ventured. "Might want to try Justin's cure first."

"You can sweat at the spa, Nat," Ellie offered. "They have hot springs and pools with different heat levels."

Lily straightened. "What time did the boys say they'd be back from racing around in the woods?"

"Five? Five-thirty?" Sarah chimed in as she entered, and all heads turned toward her. Though rumpled like the others, she sported a small grin. "Which won't give them time to whine about their sore this or that."

"How come?" Paige asked.

"Because cocktails are served at 6:30," Justin remarked, as if this was obvious to everyone. "I expect they'll need to get cleaned up first, yes? Then our special dinner is served at 7:30."

Lily's mouth twisted to one side. "Special dinner?"

"Blake and Michaela's rehearsal dinner," Paige explained in a bland tone.

"Oh!"

Michaela slumped in her seat. "There's a wedding tomorrow, remember? *My* wedding! It's the reason we're all here." And the reason a minister would be showing up during cocktail hour— someone neither Blake nor Michaela had met, who would be walking them through the ceremony tonight before marrying them tomorrow. Michaela had spent little time around people who made religion their living, and the thought intimidated her. Good thing Blake would be by her side.

Ellie reached over and patted her forearm. "Sorry, Mick. Guess we're all a little off this morning, whether it's overdoing last night or ... other stuff going on."

Other stuff. God, Michaela hoped everyone got back on track with everyone else before the wedding, or it was going to be a real downer. Too bad her bestie, Fiona, who was cruising the Mediterranean with her husband for the next month, hadn't been able to abandon ship and attend. That's what happened when one opted for a last-minute ceremony. Fiona would have been Michaela's maid of honor instead of Paige—not that Paige wasn't an outstanding substitute—but having a *happy* couple would have been a nice buttress against all the pissed-offedness charging the air. She would talk to Blake when she saw him later, and maybe tonight, when everyone was back under the same roof, they could work out some kind of truce between couples still holding grudges.

Just what I wanted to do at my wedding: be a marriage counselor. With a sigh, Michaela sipped her cocktail.

She dragged her boneless body from Paige's Escalade, impatient to rinse the smell of sulfur from her skin. Above them, snow tumbled from a black sky, and the castle's outdoor lights illuminated the curtain of snowflakes swirling around them. A storm had moved in, but they'd hardly noticed. For the past five hours, they'd been buffed, polished, and waxed, and they'd endured muscle-pounding massages and facial scraping before boiling their bodies in every hot spring on the spa's menu. The good news: Michaela's Blake-induced aches had dissolved away. The bad news: she had little idea how she would hold herself upright through the big dinner. *Strap me to a backboard.*

The rest of the women joined her, and they huddled together as they made their way to the front door.

Lily shot a glance over her shoulder. "That's weird. I don't see Gage's Range Rover."

"Or Dave's truck," Ellie added.

"Or Quinn's either. It's almost six. Weren't they supposed to be done at four?" Mia asked.

"They must have stopped off at a bar ... or a strip joint," Sarah chuckled.

Michaela's eyes virtually rolled. "Up here? Doubtful." Besides, the minister would be there in less than an hour, and it wasn't like Blake to blow off something that important. Not that he was blowing anything off ... yet. Then again, he was at the mercy of the driver of whatever vehicle he rode in.

Once inside, they shucked their coats and drifted toward the kitchen, where Justin and his crew were busy filling the place with mouth-watering aromas. Michaela's stomach rumbled in appreciation. He shooed them into a nearby family room, and Paige dropped into an armchair so large she looked like a small child whose feet barely brushed the floor. Rummaging around in her pockets, she pulled out her phone and whooshed out a breath as she looked at it. A tender smile spread across her face. She glanced up at Michaela. "Beck's sister-in-law sent me a bunch of pictures of the girls. They look like they're having so much fun. And the babies are doing great." She thumbed a text as Michaela checked her own phone. Nothing. Not a peep from Blake, even though she'd sent him a few throughout the day. The boys should have been in phone range long ago.

Michaela cocked an eyebrow at the other women, also checking their phones as they found seats in couches and chairs clustered around an enormous coffee table. "Have any of you heard from the guys?"

They all shook their heads. When she looked back at Paige, her friend had finished texting and was frowning at her device.

The floating feeling that had taken over Michaela's body after their spa day was slowly being replaced by tightening coils in her gut.

"A call from Beck from a few hours ago. It wasn't there before when I checked. Why is it just now popping up?" She muttered the last bit to herself ... and the next bit. "Can't be much of a message. It's only seventeen seconds."

Would you just listen to it already? Thistle spikes sprouted inside Michaela, poking at her. "Are you going to listen to it?" She tried to keep the sharp edge from her voice, but Paige's wide-eyed expression told her she'd failed.

Paige sat forward and fiddled with the phone. As she placed it to her ear, the other women also sat forward. Michaela leaned her arms on her thighs and dropped her head in her palms, holding her breath.

"I can't ... God, this is so hard to hear," Paige remarked while she hit something on her device. Her eyes narrowed as she listened. Then they widened and turned dark, reminding Michaela of pucks.

Paige straightened and inhaled a breath. "Oh no," she whispered. Handing the phone to Michaela, she ordered her to listen. "I'm not sure I heard right."

With shaking hands, Michaela placed the phone to her ear. A sound like howling wind came through, and with it, the faint sound of Beckett's voice. She strained to hear, then cranked up the volume and pressed the back button.

"I had the same problem," Paige murmured.

"Shush!" Michaela listened again, all her focus on Beckett's voice. The words she recognized sent icy fingers of fear skittering through her.

"Pix ... we ... avalanche ... digging ... can't find ... need help ... love you ... the girls ... so damn much."

No! Tears filled her eyes, blurring her vision as she looked up at Paige and handed the phone back. Fear furrowed Paige's brows, and she yanked the phone from Michaela's hold and tapped on a number.

"C'mon, c'mon! Pick up, pick up, pick up!" she hissed. Several breathless beats later, she tried again. "Don't do this, Beck! Pick up! Please pick up!"

Michaela bit her wobbling lip while she squelched the wail that threatened to tear from her. *Blake!*

The other women pressed in close.

"Anything?" Michaela prompted in a quavering voice, though she already knew the answer.

Paige simply shook her head.

"What's happening?" Natalie barked.

Tears trickling down her cheeks, Paige looked her in the eye before moving her gaze to every other wife or girlfriend. In a strained voice, she said, "From what I can tell, our boys were caught in an avalanche. I think they're in trouble."

Somehow hearing Paige say it out loud made the horror real, and it grabbed Michaela and shook her. She crumpled in her seat and cried out. "Oh God, no! Blake!"

Chapter 10

THE LONG GAME

*P*aige lurched to her feet, her knees threatening to liquefy and give out beneath her, vaguely aware of rising voices and commotion waving through the women gathered around her. Numbness crept up her legs, her torso, squeezing her chest so breaths were hard to come by. Her mind cried out to Beckett, searching the ether for something, anything, that would tell her he was all right.

It wasn't them. They're in a bar somewhere, drinking, laughing, comparing how they outdid each other on their snowmobiles today. Beck is just playing a really bad joke on me. Or maybe they were playing the ultimate bachelor party prank on Blake, stranding him—

Natalie's screech cut that idea short. "I can't reach T.J. either. What do we do?"

Paige snapped out of her fog, and she looked at her friends. "Have you all tried calling—"

"Yes!" they interrupted in a chorus before she could get the rest of the question out.

"I've tried Mac a half dozen times now," Mia said in a shaky voice, "but it's going straight to voicemail, like his phone is shut off. He would never shut it off. The kids—" She broke into a sob and leaned her head into Sarah, who wrapped an arm around her.

Paige lowered herself to a couch, scooped up her phone, and dialed a number she'd never called before—911.

"Park County Sheriff's Office. What is your emergency?"

"Our husbands were out snowmobiling, and they haven't come home. I got a call from mine, and it was hard to hear, but he said something about an avalanche. Has there been an avalanche?" she rambled, her words tumbling over one another in a bid to get out.

The dispatcher sounded young, hesitant, and asked her a few questions, not answering any in return. "I'll relay the information, and someone will be in touch," the girl said and hung up before Paige could stop her.

What. The. Hell!

In a clipped staccato, Paige filled in the others. As she was preparing to dial 911 once more, her phone rang with an unfamiliar number.

A man's brusque voice greeted her when she answered. "Paige Miller?"

"This is she. Are you from 911? I'm trying to find out if there's been an avalanche."

"This is Larry Gilbert from Park County Search and Rescue. You have a lost party?"

Panic flared inside her at the words "search and rescue." "Yes. Has there been an avalanche?" she repeated.

"Maybe we should start with you telling me about your lost party?"

"Who are you again?" She snapped her fingers, and Sarah grabbed a pen and paper and shoved them at her.

The man's voice remained even. "Larry Gilbert. I'm the Incident Commander for Search and Rescue. We work under the Park County Sheriff's Office, and Dispatch contacted us, saying you have a lost party. I'm calling to get the details."

"Oh. Oh!" While all eyes fastened on her, Paige put a stranglehold on her annoyance, her fear, and her embarrassment over acting like a dolt. Haltingly, she told the commander everything she knew. She ended on an assumptive close. "How soon can you start looking for them?"

He blew past her question with one of his own. "Have you contacted the company they rented the snowmobiles from?"

Paige looked helplessly at a panic-stricken Ellie. "Who did Dave rent the snowmobiles from?"

"I don't know!" Ellie wailed.

"There are only a half dozen or so outfits around here, so I suggest you start by calling them," the IC said.

"Aren't they closed now?"

"Probably not. They'll be sorting and stocking gear for tomorrow."

"Can't you just go out and *look*?" Paige pleaded.

"Ma'am, we haven't confirmed they truly are missing. And where would you have us start?" His thinly veiled sarcasm—or what her reeling mind took for sarcasm—made her clench her fist; she wanted to reach through the phone and throttle him. "Our county covers a lot of territory. We can't just send out ground teams without *some* idea where to search."

"What about an air search?" She heard the rising alarm in her own voice.

"Impossible in this storm. The winds are too high."

"Wait. So you won't be looking for them tonight?" *They could freeze to death!*

He sighed. "I cannot jeopardize my field people by sending them out in these conditions, *especially* when I have no idea where to send them or if there is a need."

Paige pushed a breath through her lungs, trying to keep herself and her voice calm. "So our only option is to start calling snowmobile rental places? Then what? *They* track our men down?"

"I've got it!" Ellie yelled, looking at her phone. "I just checked our credit card charges, and there's one to Pinnacle Adventures."

"Pinnacle Adventures," Paige shouted into the phone. "Do they rent snowmobiles?"

"Hang on." Shuffling noises told her the IC had covered his mic. When he was back, his tone had sobered further. "Ma'am, I want you to call Pinnacle and find out if their snowmobiles have been returned. That's step one. Step two, you call me back and let me know what you find out. In the meantime, I need your name, the name of everyone in your missing party, and best contact information. What time did that call come in from your husband?" Something in his voice had Paige's already raw edges fraying further. And though his manner had rubbed her until static crackled, she didn't want to lose the connection—something told her he was a lifeline to Beckett.

"What?" Mia hissed. "What are they saying?"

Paige held up her finger and looked at Ellie. "Call Pinnacle," she whispered, "and ask if they got their snowmobiles back. Hurry!"

With one ear, she listened to Ellie while she fielded the IC's questions with the other. As he was about to hang up, she darted a hopeful gaze to Ellie and mouthed, "Anything?"

The color had drained from Ellie's face. She nodded at Paige and thanked whomever she spoke to on the phone, then handed it off to Sarah with a directive. "Give them our contact information." She scurried to Paige's side, tears glossing her eyes. "The boys picked up the snowmobiles as planned this morning, but they haven't returned them yet."

"Oh dear God!" Lily cried.

Ellie ran on, her voice quavering. "They told them where to park and gave them maps that showed what trails to follow. When the guys didn't show up, someone from the rental place went to the trailhead but didn't find any of their vehicles. They checked with some of the other people who were riding today, but no one saw them." She pulled in a sharp breath. "There's more."

Paige's heart slammed against her rib cage. "Commander, are you hearing this?" Her voice slid into high-pitch territory without her permission.

"I'm listening," came his reply.

Ellie, looking like she might burst into tears at any moment, continued. "A mechanic who works on the snowmobiles said that one of our boys, and I'm guessing it's Dave, showed a lot of interest in some area that's off the beaten path about twenty miles from where they were supposed to be. It's a place locals sometimes go, but it's not part of the trail system where they normally send the tourists."

"Did she say twenty miles from the trailhead?" the IC asked.

Paige put him on speaker. "A place locals go that's twenty miles away, right?" she repeated to Ellie.

"Yes," Ellie answered. "He also said the mechanic warned our guy—it had to be Dave—not to go there." Ellie paused to lower her voice. "But if I know Dave—"

"I think I know the spot," the IC said. "Dangerous backcountry, especially this time of year."

"Is there a chance they might have gotten caught in an avalanche?" Sarah gaped, wide-eyed.

"Paige?" the IC's voice boomed. "Can you take me off speaker?"

She frowned her confusion at the other women but did as he asked. "Okay, Commander. You're off speaker now."

"You'll be at this number?"

The hairs on the back of her neck pricked up. "Yes, of course. But I feel like you're not telling me something. What's going on?"

A few beats passed, as if he was deliberating. "I've been checking since we've been on the phone. The CAIC—that's the Colorado Avalanche Information Center—got a report earlier today of an avalanche in that same area." Paige gasped, and the IC's tone softened. "Now the person who called it in scanned with binoculars and said he didn't see anyone, so there's a very good chance your men weren't anywhere near there, okay?"

A slippery, queasy feeling took up residence in Paige's stomach. "Did anyone search after the avalanche?"

"No, and that's normal when we don't have any reports of people being involved. Now, Paige, I want you to stay calm, stay by your phone, and if your men come waltzing through the door, or if you get a phone call or a text from any of them, one of you needs to call me immediately, you understand?"

"Y-yes."

"I want you to write down my details. If we don't know where your men are by morning when I go off shift, someone will relay contact information for tomorrow's incident commander, understood?"

"Morning?" she choked out, her mind rocketing to Beckett alone in the cold. Did he have food? Water? Had he dressed warmly enough that morning? *No idea. I made sure he was gone before I got up because I was still mad at him.* Exactly why she'd been mad escaped her.

A stab at her chest had her drawing in a strangled breath.

"Paige, I understand how difficult it is for families waiting for word about their loved ones," he soothed. "But I need *you* to be *my* IC on your end, you got that?"

Just then, Natalie declared, "Maybe we should rent our own snowmobiles and go looking for them!"

"And where do we get those lights they use for night skiing?" Sarah added from behind her, followed by Mia, who offered a more logical solution. "I think we want headlamps. You know, the kind you strap on your head."

"Will they rent any this late? In this weather?" Lily posed.

Michaela's gaze traveled around the room. "I don't think going out tonight is a good—"

"Paige?" The IC's voice in her ear pulled her back to the conversation she was supposed to be having with him. "Whatever you do, do not—I repeat, do *not*—let your friends get it in their heads to go searching. All they're going to do is make double work for us and hamper any effort to locate your men ... assuming we even have to, that is. There's still a chance they'll come home any minute. Understood?"

Michaela's reassuring hand landed on her shoulder, its calming effect a lifeline Paige grasped on to. She cleared her throat. "Understood."

The IC seemed to breathe a sigh of relief. "Good. Now write this down."

Though Paige wrote down everything Larry Gilbert dictated and gave him information on their missing men, the cold, hard fact that Beckett wasn't there became her entire focus. Would she ever see his smiling face walking through the door again, see that twinkle is in his big blue eyes when he prowled toward her?

Fear, cold and leaden, filled every nook and cranny in her heart until it was brittle.

When she hung up, she took in the pale, grave faces surrounding her and knew she wasn't the only one on the verge of descending into full-on despair. Michaela's hand still gripped her shoulder. "Deep breaths, everyone," Paige said in a surprisingly calm voice. "We don't know if they were caught up in the avalanche. We don't even know if they were *there*."

"And if they were?" Ellie's voice was part wail, part whimper.

"Then we need to be strong so we can help them, okay? We'll get through this. So will they." Paige bobbed her head firmly and linked hands with Ellie and Michaela, who sat on either side of her.

Mia added they should all think positive thoughts, that they didn't have enough information, but her quavering voice told Paige she didn't believe what she was trying to sell.

Paige excused herself and dashed to her bedroom, shutting the door behind her. Re-cueing Beckett's message, she listened to his tinny voice scratching its way through the air. When the voicemail reached the part where he told her he loved her and the girls, she couldn't hold back the sobs.

An arrow to the heart.

Wrapping herself around a pillow, she sent out a missive to the universe.

I'm so, so sorry, Beck. Please come back to me, to us. We need you. I need you. I love you so much.

Chapter 11

What Are we Rehearsing?

A loud bing-bonging reverberated in Natalie's already murky brain, and she looked up from where she sat beside Lily to see Justin presenting a woman cloaked head to toe in winter duds. The woman pulled off a beanie, shaking snow from it, and offered them a tentative smile.

Except for Paige, they all still sat in the room, numbed by the news. Michaela seemed to come to, and she jumped up and made a beeline for the woman while Lily looked on glumly. Not a word had been exchanged between them since Paige had fled to her bedroom minutes before. They had been suspended in shock, in a shared fog of silence, and that silence sat heavily on Natalie's shoulders—like the snow that might be pressing in on T.J. right now.

Where are you?

Her primal side strained to jump into the Audi and scour the pines lining the highway, to tear the damn forest apart looking for him. Her logical side held just enough sway to talk her down, and she found herself in a constant state of battle that did little to rescue her man.

The knot that had formed in her chest since they'd discovered the boys were in danger hadn't slipped even a fraction of a millimeter. If anything, it had grown bigger and twisted in on itself, like a pretzeling boa constrictor.

Was he out there, injured and cold? Was he freezing to death? Was he alive? Of course he was. He *had* to be. Her man was the toughest of the tough, a powerful, invincible warrior.

Why was I so mean to him? Why didn't I tell him how much I love him?

All the plans they'd made, the dreams they'd shared ... they had so many yet to achieve together.

An inadvertent sob sneaked its way past her throat. Lily reached over and squeezed Natalie's hand in a silent display of support and shared sorrow.

Oh God! Lily! She's already been widowed once, and she has two young children! How could I be so self-absorbed? I'm not the only one suffering here.

Natalie squeezed back—hard. Then she swung her attention to Michaela, who seemed to be apologizing to the woman still in her winter gear. The woman, in turn, had placed her hand on Michaela's upper arm in a way that suggested she was offering comfort. Bits of their conversation floated back to Natalie. Her confusion cleared, and she realized this stranger was the minister who was supposed to marry Michaela and Blake tomorrow! Dear God, this was the eve of Michaela's wedding, the night of the rehearsal dinner. Not that anyone could eat right now. But they should have been looking forward to sucking down Chef Justin's food, toasting, laughing, celebrating *with* their men, unlike last night when a cold curtain had separated the men from the women ... a curtain Natalie had been more than guilty of helping construct.

The minister offered to stay, but when Michaela thanked her and told her it wasn't necessary, she wished them all luck, promised them prayers, and left. It occurred to Natalie that the minister's offer of help might be necessary—they needed all the heavenly help they could get right now.

Michaela returned and took a seat beside Natalie, snuggling close. With confidence she didn't possess, Natalie patted her hand and softly said, "It'll be okay, Mick. They'll come home, and we'll celebrate that wedding."

Michaela sniffled and dabbed at wet cheeks with the hem of her sweater. "Thanks, Nat. And T.J. will come through that door and toss you in the air like he always does."

They choked out a shared laugh at T.J.'s antics. Natalie wasn't small, but he liked to manhandle her as though she weighed no more than one of their pups ... probably his own way of showing off his He-Man strength, which she absolutely loved about him.

She sagged against Michaela's arm on a sigh. "We fought about having kids. It seemed so monumental at the time, so insurmountable, but now? I just want the big lug home where I can hug him and tell him how much I love him."

"What about the kids issue?" Lily gently asked.

Tears sprang to Natalie's eyes, and she swiped at them angrily with the heel of her hand. "Being with him is what matters. Kids matter too, but if he were here right now, I'd tell him I'm willing to put off having them until he's ready, whenever that might be. Well, hopefully before I'm sixty so I don't have to have some kind of implant or something." Though Lily gave her an indulgent smile, Natalie's attempt at humor fell way short. Nothing was funny about this nightmare.

Anguish welled inside her, wedging in her chest and her throat, making it difficult to breathe. She turned into Lily's shoulder and cried.

"I don't want to lose him."

Natalie's words punched breath from Lily's lungs. She'd been trying to hold it together, but darkness and dread were moving in, taking over, snuffing out hope. She'd been in these shadowy corners before; never had she imagined traveling back to this hell, stuck on the river Styx with no way to jump out of the boat taking her farther and farther into inky nothingness.

What had she and Gage argued about? His mother. The poor guy was constantly walking the line between her and Lily. Had he deserved Lily's scornful blast? And was the conflict so monumental that she'd needed to expend every ounce of energy ignoring him last night? Not when she should have been curled up in his arms, making love to him, telling him with her words and showing him with her body that he was her world.

God, he was the best man she'd ever known. Somehow she'd struck the jackpot, and he'd picked *her* out of all the women he could have had. An old soul with a huge heart who never hid his adoration for her and their kids, who shared all he was with everyone he cared about, even the more difficult people in his life ... like his mother, whom Lily wasn't sure deserved all he gave. But that was Gage, and Lily should have cheered him on, told him how wonderful and patient he was, supported him when dealing with his mom wasn't easy for him either. Been his friend, his ally, his safe harbor. Instead, she'd stormed all over him for being a loving son. The very traits that made him a loving son also made him the loving husband and father she adored.

Flames flickered cheerfully in a huge stone fireplace, and she stared, mesmerized by their colorful dance. But she saw only bleakness in their bright display. Closing her eyes, she sent out a silent plea that God or an angel or her long-dead first husband—anyone who might be listening—carry a message to the man who filled her heart and whom she couldn't live without.

One more chance, Gage. Please. I need to let you know you are my world and you always will be.

Please don't leave me.

Sarah sat quietly in a leather armchair, her eyes fastened on the intricate swirls in the huge area rug—was that a Turkish rug? It didn't matter. Nothing mattered but getting Quinn home.

She was vaguely aware that Lily, Michaela, and Natalie huddled together on the couch perpendicular to her chair and that Mia sat in the chair beside hers. They were amorphous blobs topped with different shades and textures of hair.

And though she was as still and silent as a statue, her mind was as noisy as a hive filled with angry bees. In her lap, her curled fingers were laced together so tightly she had to remind herself to relax every time they went numb.

As for what filled her mind's movie screen, all she saw, all she *wanted* to see, was Quinn's handsome face split in his trademark mischievous grin—the one that popped his dimples. His long-lashed, cocoa-colored eyes swept over her in that sexy, sultry way he had. That look could mean anything from "Your clothes are coming off in the next ten seconds, Sunshine" to "Don't you want to bake me a batch of chocolate chip cookies because I'm so fucking cute?" to "Sit back and be amazed by my juggling prowess." At times, he was unreadable like that, but when it truly counted, like when he was telling her with his eyes how much he loved her, his every thought was as readable as the romance novels on her e-reader.

She'd studied that face thousands of times, and still her tummy fluttered every time she saw it. She *loved* that face, just as she loved the man it belonged to ... the one she could talk to for hours about the construction of a dome on an eighteenth-century capitol building or who made her laugh despite a blue mood—not that she had them often, thanks to him. No, with him she soared to heights she'd never thought possible before. She'd always been independent, but somehow being with him enhanced that in her, made her more complete, more *her*. Logically, it didn't add up, yet it worked somehow, like so many things with him, and she'd stopped trying to sort it logically a long time ago. With him, she could simply *be*; she could breathe; she could be more of who she was. Because as much as she loved him, he loved her back without reserve. It was an intoxicating, liberating, wondrous thing she would never find with anyone else.

And it was the possibility of missing that feeling of wholeness that most terrified her whenever she contemplated life without Quinn ... like now.

Sarah prided herself on being tough. Stoic. Bullet-proof. But her husband and her brother were missing, and she was a gooey jumble inside, trying to hold it all in before it spilled from her in an ugly mess.

All Quinn had wanted was to spend Christmas alone, with *her*. Damn, how sweet was that? And she'd acted like he had asked her to give a gallon of blood in one sitting. Yes, her mother might be facing Christmas without either of her children, but she'd sort of had it coming to her for years. And it wasn't as if she'd be alone—she had plenty of friends. Shouldn't Sarah's loyalty have automatically aligned itself with her husband?

Funny how clear it all seemed *now*. Why hadn't she had that crystal clarity when Quinn had first balked? He hadn't done it because he didn't get along with her mom—Nola, like most women on the planet, could not resist Quinn Charming.

Yeah, Sarah was regretting the way she'd sprung the idea on him. She should have soft-pedaled the notion instead of dropping a bombshell on him right before they arrived for what was supposed to be a romantic getaway. Better yet, she should have broken the bad news to Nola ages ago. Instead, she'd blindsided unsuspecting Quinn. And last night when he'd offered an olive branch after dinner? God, she'd been a total bitch and told him she preferred being with her girlfriends to spending time in the same room with him. He'd surprised her when he hadn't joined her in bed—it was the first time since they'd been together—but then again, would she have joined *him* if he'd said something equally venomous to her?

Nope.

God, for a do-over. *That's all I want. A chance to make things right, to let him know how much I love him.*

Sarah wasn't alone in her misery. She'd lost track of Ellie, but in her peripheral vision, Mia swiped at tears moistening her cheeks, and Sarah's heart shattered for her. For them all.

Mia wasn't officially Mac's kids' mom yet, but they sure looked at her that way. What would happen to them? What would become of Mia? How would she explain ...?

No, the boys are all right. They're out there somewhere, and they're all fine, and they'll all come home, and there will be some big joke, and we'll want to wring their necks, but we'll all have a great time at the wedding tomorrow.

Would they all come home, though? Were they alive?

What if some make it and some don't? Like drawing straws. Will I be jumping for joy or crumpling into a blubbering heap? And if I'm jumping for joy, am I doing it in front of one of us whose other half didn't make it?

God, I don't know if you're up there, but if you are, please, please, please bring Quinn home. I need my Sparky.

Ellie paced ... and paced ... and paced. Like a prowling, penned-up cat with energy it needed to expend, striding to and fro. She was in a sitting area off the family room where the rest of the girls sat, unable to be part of them yet not willing to be without them. They were *all* suffering, but she had no comfort for them—not when she was desperately trying to comfort herself.

Her arms ached to hold Kelsey, but they ached a little more to hold Dave close to her, to feel his solid heat against her, to feel his powerful arms engulfing her while he kissed her hair and spoke soothing words in her ear. He didn't even have to say much ... simply the sound of his voice rumbling through his granite chest had the ability to loosen the too-tight bands that often gripped her. Was that love she felt for him or was it dependence? Or both? Was it healthy? She didn't know, didn't care. It was the way it was, their dynamic, and he seemed to relish taking care of her and their baby as much as she reveled in that care.

The big, burly badass had a softness about him when it came to her and their daughter, and he didn't mind letting it show. Everyone *knew* she and Kelsey were the most important fixtures in Dave's life.

How surprising was that? And how surprising was it that she'd seamlessly transitioned from independent businesswoman to homemaker and mom? Something about that easy switch brought up a boatload of guilt inside her. Friends from her former life still worked. Hell, most of them had kids *and* jobs outside the home, and they didn't mind telling her how lucky she was to have a husband who made gobs of money and kept her home.

No, that wasn't right. He didn't *keep* her home or anywhere she didn't choose to be, nor did he keep her from doing anything she wanted. The simple truth was she *was* doing what she wanted, though saying so aloud made her somewhat of a dinosaur, a throwback to a 1960s sitcom. June Cleaver, minus the standard-issue pearls, dress, and heels. Taking care of him, their home, and their daughter filled a void she had never been cognizant of before. Was it so terrible to *not* want to be Superwoman and do it all? She already had it all. Wasn't that enough?

Maybe her reluctance at having a second child had more to do with feeling entrenched in the homemaker role when the women she surrounded herself with, like Paige—whom she looked up to and tried to emulate—*were* superwomen. She had convinced herself she was inferior somehow, that she should share their ambitions and strive to be powerhouses like them. Yet wasn't she a powerhouse in her own right?

Maybe she needed to come to terms with the new Ellie, the one who loved her life the way it was. Maybe it was time to banish the feelings of inadequacy and guilt.

Paige flew into the family room, startling the other women. "Where's Ellie?"

Ellie stiffened in the shadows. "Right here, Paige." She headed into the soft, golden light in the family room. Wide eyes followed her the entire way. When she drew up beside Paige, she registered the phone in Paige's trembling hands.

"Search and Rescue just sent me a picture," Paige began haltingly. "I thought I recognized it as Dave's truck but wanted to check with you first."

Ellie pulled in a heavy breath, bracing herself to see a mangled wreck. In those few beats, thoughts bombarded her brain. Had she lost Dave, her man, her rock? What would she tell Kelsey as she grew up? *That her daddy loved her beyond measure.* He loved that little girl with a fierceness that was simultaneously laugh-provoking and so endearing it turned Ellie's heart to something resembling the contents of an overheated fondue pot. He doted on and poured his entire heart into his family, off *and* on the ice. He was the perfect teammate, the perfect dad, the perfect husband. Men like him should be fathers to lots of children. What had she been so afraid of before?

Her eyes strayed to Paige's phone screen, and the breath she'd held fled from her. Dave's pristine truck was intact, with his empty snowmobile trailer attached. Nothing looked out of place, except that it was parked in a snow-covered field, it was nighttime, and he wasn't in the picture.

Her heart accelerated. "Yes, that's it. Where did they find it? Have they found the guys?"

Paige held up her index finger. "Larry, did you hear that?"

"I did," replied the IC. "And the other vehicles?"

Paige turned her head toward Lily, who had risen from the couch. Wordlessly, Paige swiped to a different picture, and Lily gasped as she looked on from over Paige's shoulder.

Tears sprang into her big blue eyes. "That's Gage's Range Rover."

Sarah joined them, craning her head over Paige's other shoulder as the latter swiped her device once more. "Definitely Quinn's truck."

"Okay," Larry's voice sounded through the speaker. "The vehicles are parked near the area we talked about."

"Meaning what?" Ellie blurted.

"That's Ellie Grimson," Paige explained, "the wife of Dave Grimson, one of the men whose truck and trailer we just identified."

"The Grim Reaper? From the Blizzard?" came Larry's startled voice. Another voice in the background piped up. "Oh shit! He's my favorite player!"

Ellie exchanged glances with Paige. In any other situation, they would have burst into laughter. Instead, Paige's mouth thinned to a hard line as she stared at the phone she held in a crushing grip.

A throat clear and Larry returned to his no-nonsense tone. "The Range Rover belongs to Gage Nelson, I take it?"

"Yes," Lily squeaked.

"Okay," Larry continued. "We have a good idea where to begin our search in the morning. The storm is supposed to let up by daybreak. Assuming that's the case, we'll have a helicopter with what we call our 'hasty team,' along with dogs, in the air and searching at first light. We'll find your men."

Breath stuttered in Ellie's chest. *We'll find your men.* The question was, would they find them in time?

As she stood beside the players' wives who hugged one another and held on, Mia's mind leapt with joy, pulling her mood from the deep morass where it had been floundering. Where for hours she'd pondered the futility of finding the men in such a vast wilderness—in the dark, during a storm—the fact that Search and Rescue now had a starting point shone hope like a bright beacon.

Her thoughts returned to Mac and his kids. Had Mia made the right call by not telling his parents? By not telling his kids? She didn't know. All she knew was that Mac was lost out in the freezing cold somewhere and that ignorance bubble surrounding his parents and kids was a bliss she wished she could share. The torment of not knowing, of imagining everything that could be happening to him, wasn't anything she wanted to burden them with. Besides, what was her rightful role in all of this? As a wife, the lines were clearly marked. But as a fiancée? What were the rules? Had she earned the same level of recognition as these wives she stood among? And honestly, who besides her was even concerned about the lack of a marriage license in her virtual vault?

She stole a glance at Michaela, whose eyes seemed to have an unbroken sheen of tears since Paige had first talked to Search and Rescue and reality had slammed into all of them. Michaela was in the same boat as Mia ... or maybe not since tomorrow was to have been her wedding day. She and Blake lived together, acted every bit like husband and wife, and tomorrow ... Well, whenever they got married, the act would simply be a formality.

With Mia and Mac, the situation was different. Mia didn't live with him and the kids—her rule, not his—and they hadn't set a wedding date. Also her doing. The question spinning in her mind was: Why? Why had she set the boundaries? Mac certainly had no qualms about her moving in. And while her moving in with Mac wouldn't have been her parents' first choice, they loved Mac and were glad Mia had found her "one." They would never pass judgment. The kids didn't think in terms of legitimate license— they simply wanted her there, and like their father, they held nothing back. They were ready to love her like she was their mom. Correction: they already did, and she loved them right back.

So what was she afraid of?

Failure.

She'd used poor judgment before. What was to say it didn't have her in its clutches now? But when she examined that argument with logic rather than fear, it didn't hold up. Mac was the complete package, as steadfast at home as he was in the net. The guys loved him. Everyone loved him. Loving him was as easy as ... It was easy. So easy, in fact, that maybe she'd invented an issue where one didn't exist.

From the couch, Michaela sniffled, her face a soggy mess of misery. "I should be sleeping right now, dreaming about my wedding tomorrow—I guess it's today already, isn't it?—and pledging myself forever to my fairy-tale prince. But instead, I'm curled up on a couch with my girlfriends, all of us sick with worry about our men and helpless to do anything to bring them home. I may never get that perfect sunset exit into Happily-Ever-After-Land with the man of my dreams." Sobbing, she fell into Sarah's embrace, and Mia's heart splintered for her ... for them ... for herself. Mostly for herself because as terrifying as committing to a real wedding date was, the thought of being without Mac the rest of her life was exponentially worse. How would she survive without him?

Mac, if you're out there, please come home. I will marry you on the spot. We'll make it a double wedding! She nearly chuckled aloud but got herself under control.

Just come home so I can tell you what you mean to me and how much I want our life together.

Chapter 12

HUDDLE AND CUDDLE

Beckett yanked at the zipper of his jacket, but it was as closed as it was going to get. Though he knew this, it didn't keep him from trying ... again. He stuffed his hand back in his glove, then tucked it under his armpit, grateful he had *some* sensation in his fingers. Not so his nose, his toes, or his ass. Maybe not feeling the latter was a blessing since it pressed into ground littered with jagged chunks of decomposing granite. Jesus, he was cold! *But*, he reminded himself, *at least I'm in one piece and* know *I'm cold*. Huddled in a ball, he pressed a little closer to Shanstrom, who was sandwiched between him and a sleeping Nelson. At least he *hoped* Nelson was sleeping. They were taking turns playing monkey in the middle to ward off the chill in their space-blanket snow fort. Nelson kept drifting off, and while Beckett wasn't up on his winter survival skills, a voice in his head told him falling asleep in freezing temperatures was a bad, bad thing.

"Is Nelson breathing?" he asked.

Nelson kicked his foot in response.

"Good to know." *And at least I felt that*. Apprehension spiked as his mind turned to a different member of their party: Blake Barrett. Dude hadn't been in great shape when they'd hauled him out of his snow grave, and since he was being tended to by the rest of their group in a different makeshift shelter, Beckett had no clue how he was doing. An image of Barrett's gray-blue face swam in Beckett's mind, and he told himself—again—there was nothing they could do but wait out the night and hope for a miraculous outcome.

His mind then wandered to Michaela, and his heart sank lower in his chest. What if Blake didn't make it? Which one of them would deliver the awful news? What would she do? *Fall to pieces.* She'd been on the verge of marrying the man she had planned to spend the rest of her life with, for fuck's sake. This was supposed to be a time filled with happiness and flowers. How would she survive the loss?

"You think Barrett's going to be okay?" Beckett choked out.

Shanny grunted.

"Was that a yes, a no, or a 'don't get so fucking close'?"

"It was an 'I can't feel my fucking lips so stop asking me stupid damn questions'!" Shanstrom snapped.

Grateful for the distraction, Beckett retorted, "Even more important that you talk, then, so they don't freeze from lack of circulation and fall off. Not having lips makes it all kinds of hard when you go to kiss your wife." *And I'll go fucking insane if I don't hear a human voice. Something besides my hammering heart or the flapping cover or wolves howling.* Not that there were any wolves howling—yet. Only the wind howled outside their makeshift shelter, which was nothing more than four short walls of compacted snow covered by a space blanket they'd crawled under. Ironic that their only protection from the sub-freezing temperatures was a thin sheet of Mylar and ... snow.

No one knew where they were. They were too far from where they'd started, in an area they never should have gone, without enough survival gear to go around. Just two space blankets, a collapsible bowl, and a box of ancient matches—not that they could get a fire started in this weather anyway.

Long gone were the stale protein bars and water bottles—the unfrozen ones—that had been in Grimson's pack. They'd divided those up after realizing the remnants of their lunch cooler had been swept away by the avalanche. As for the meager contents of

Grimson's flask, Grimson had doled it out to Barrett, who now lay in the other shelter somewhere near the one where Beckett huddled with Shanstrom and Nelson.

Shanny's dark voice startled Beckett back to their shared igloo. "Well, not having my fingers and toes is going to make all kinds of everything hard to do."

"Speaking of hard, at least your pecker is staying warm, so you'll still have it. Natalie will appreciate that, even if your lips and fingers don't work."

"Damn, you're as funny as a rubber crutch, Miller."

"Now you sound like my wife."

Shanny shuffled beside him, their jackets slipping against each other with a nylon squeak. "Can I ask you both something?"

"Sure, I'm happy to stick around and take questions. Got nowhere else to be," Beckett said dryly. Nelson merely huffed.

"When you got married, did you know you wanted kids?"

Nelson coughed a "Yep."

The answer tumbled from Beckett's lips without him having to formulate it. "I knew it *before* I married her."

"No doubt in your mind?" Shanstrom said.

"No doubt in my mind."

Shanny craned his head, and one eye gleamed in the dark from inside his hood. "*How* did you know?"

Beckett sighed, wrestling with whether to divulge the secret he and Andie shared. As snow pressed against his neck and back, it struck him that the sanctity of the secret wouldn't matter if they didn't survive the night, and there was a *high* probability they wouldn't survive. "She got pregnant ... before."

He felt T.J. jerk beside him. "When she was married to that asshole?"

"No. When she and I ... well, when things went from the friend zone to the hot zone."

"Fuck, I'd like some of that hot zone right about now."

"You mean things aren't so good between you and Natalie?" Beckett didn't hide his surprise. His buddy from way back might be all kinds of stoic, but when it came to Natalie, he'd never been

103

able to hide much. The otherwise tough guy lit up like a Christmas tree every time she walked into a room ... kind of like how Andie affected Beckett.

Yeah, like that.

"No, not that. I was trying to make a joke about our predicament. Hot zone. Get it?"

Beckett groaned. "I do now, unfortunately. You do know it's not a joke when you have to explain it, right?"

Nelson grunted his agreement.

"So about you and Paige, er, Andie," Shanny prompted, ignoring Beckett's barb. "I didn't know you got her pregnant. What happened?"

To this day, I'm not sure I got her pregnant. But he wasn't going there, freezing-to-death confession or not. "She, ah, lost the baby." Shit, and there came a stinging in his eyes. Going back to those dark, devastating places when they hadn't been together still got him. Every. Damn. Time. Losing the baby had been bad enough, but not having Andie in his life had been the hardest thing he'd ever done, bar none, and something he never wanted to experience again.

"Oh man, that sucks, dude," Nelson mumbled in the dark.

"Shit, I'm sorry," Shanny agreed.

Beckett sniffed. "Yeah, so to your point, though the pregnancy was a surprise, once I got over the shock, I was really excited about becoming a dad."

"Think you would have felt that way with anyone else?"

Another quick answer he didn't need to ponder. "No way," he chuckled. "I guess part of the reason I was so excited was because it was Andie." She had made all the difference, making him want things he'd never known he'd wanted. "I'd never thought about having kids before—hell, I couldn't even see myself married—but I realized then I wanted a future with her, and that future included kids. It was real simple."

When Shanny didn't reply, Beckett nudged his shoulder. "What about you and Nat? Any kids in your future? You've got your dogs, but—"

"So your jab earlier ..."

"What jab?"

"About me and Natalie not being in the hot zone. There's some truth to that. When we drove up yesterday—shit, was that yesterday?"

"Maybe two days ago now," Nelson offered. "A little tough to check the time when our phones don't work."

"Why don't any of us wear a fucking watch anymore?" Beckett huffed.

"Uh, pretty sure we decided to leave them behind to avoid losing them while we snowmobiled," Nelson offered.

"Kinda tough to go back and look for your Rolex in the snow," Shanny added.

Between their phones constantly searching for signal in the middle of nowhere and the damn cold, their batteries had been drained dry hours ago. And God, could they use them now—flashlight app, GPS locator, anything to give them hope in this endless night they found themselves stuck in.

Wonder if Andie got my voicemail? Shit, I wish I could talk to her right now. I'd tell her I'm okay, even if I'm not. I hate for my girl to worry.

"Anyway, we argued on the way up here," Shanny continued.

"You too? So did we."

"We did too. About what?" This muffled comment came from Nelson.

"Damned if I know," Beckett replied. "Her being busy, me being busy. I was probably whining about her not tripping over me every time I snap my fingers. Pretty sure I pouted like my oldest kid." Had any of it mattered? No. What mattered was he loved her more than life itself; she *was* his life. Her and the girls. They were his reason for breathing, for existing. Fuck the coaching job. Fuck everything but what he had already. All he needed was at home ... if he could get back there.

"You *snap* your fingers?" Nelson chortled.

"Figure of speech, dumbass. I do *not* snap my fingers at my wife."

Shanny shook his head. "No kidding. She'd probably dig her nails into your balls and make you scream. Not in a good way."

"Is there a *good* way for a chick to dig her nails into your balls?" Nelson was sounding more animated, which Beckett took as a sign the guy wasn't on death's doorstep just yet.

"I had a girl do that once," Beckett blurted. *Just keep talking. It'll help us all stay alive.*

"What?" Shanny and Nelson chorused.

"Dig her nails into my balls. Had one bite me too. Christ, did that hurt!"

Shanny guffawed. "Did you deserve it?"

"Probably. It was during my drug haze days. I was so fucked up back then." He shivered, and it wasn't only from the weather. "Thank fuck those days are long behind me."

And thank Christ I'm with a woman who understands me and who gives a fuck. Who smells like honeysuckle and tastes like its nectar and who's soft and so damn sweet I get a toothache just kissing her. Beckett had had a lot of women, but after Andie, none remained in his memory banks. They became one big blur, like wet paint in a rainstorm. Everything ran together, turned to gray, until only his pixie remained. That tiny woman did more to anchor him to this earth than he ever would have imagined. And he thanked God for her.

He swiped at a stray tear or five. Fuck, he needed to get back to her so he could hold her and tell her, so he could keep her safe. Her and their girls. Wasn't that his most important job as a man? Fueled by the cold, a circuitous and illogical thought struck him that keeping them safe was the only way *he* would be safe.

Not that it would help him out here much.

So why had he acted the way he had? He cringed as the day of their arrival came drifting back. He'd been an asshole because he'd had a tough week? She'd had a tough week too. Why hadn't he been man enough to simply take her hand and prod one of her brilliant smiles from her instead? One thing he knew for sure: if he'd pulled his head out of his ass, he would have slept curled around her instead of on the game room floor, and right now, he'd have a hell of a cozy memory warming him through this bleak night.

"Jesus, I was an utter dick," he confessed to the dark. "I wouldn't even open her damn car door."

"You sure as hell didn't hesitate opening *my* wife's car door," Nelson said.

"Compensating for being so fucking petty, I guess. I can see Andie now at my grave: 'Thanks for not opening my door, asshole.'"

Shanstrom let out a harsh laugh. "Can't say I picture Paige doing that. Pretty sure you don't either."

"Not so you could hear." *No, she wouldn't even think it—she's not built that way.* Unlike Beckett, she had a heart so big she fit everyone in it without batting her long eyelashes and still had room left over. *She'd be comforting my family and the girls, holding everything together. The girls. Fuck, will they miss me? Maybe Laynie and Audrey, but the twins? They don't even know me.*

Despair knifed into him.

Who will take care of them?

Despite huddling between two big bodies, T.J. was freezing ... and hungry ... and thirsty ... and pretty damn sure he would not make it out alive if they didn't get help.

He'd built the two shelters they hunkered in, but they needed more than snow-packed walls and flimsy Mylar tarps. They needed to get out of their damn arctic tombs. They needed heat and food and medical attention.

Dying of cold wouldn't be the worst way to go, but dying without seeing Natalie again? Without being able to push his fingers through her silky hair? Without losing himself in the depths of her beautiful amber eyes, eyes filled with so much love he was laid bare? Leaving her the way he had, with them arguing about having kids—a promise he *had* made her—leveled him inside. Crushed him. And he couldn't even text her or write a note to say how sorry he was. To say how much he loved her.

And Jesus fucking Christ, did he love her, this woman who loved *him* full-out despite the minefield of his past fuck-ups. She'd seen past it, to something buried beneath that he'd never suspected lived inside of him. She'd dug and uncovered the man he was under all the bullshit, and he'd become that man with her. And damn proud of it too, even if he didn't deserve her. Where would he be without her? She could have had anyone she wanted, yet she'd picked him, damaged goods and all. He owed her everything—the life he'd come to know and love.

Here he'd spent the better part of their short marriage hoping she didn't wake the hell up and leave his ass, yet he'd been managing to push her away all by himself, bit by bit, because he was too chickenshit to follow through on his pledge.

Nelson broke into his careening thoughts. "So what did you and Natalie fight about?"

T.J. glared at him, even though he couldn't see it. It was too cramped, too dark.

"Let me guess," Miller cut in. "You fought about having kids, didn't you?"

T.J. sent him a glare too. "What makes you say that?" Had Natalie confided in Paige?

Miller shrugged. "Guessed from the questions you asked. Plus, I know a little something about your past, and you've probably convinced yourself you're not dad material."

"You got that right." Suddenly, Natalie's words came whipping back at him. *Look how you are with the dogs. Look how you are with me. How you are with your teammates' kids and the tiny fans who swarm you. And look at your sister. She turned it around. Don't you want kids like your nephews someday?* Natalie had a way of casting everything in a positive light.

How did she do that anyway? See through him and into him? How did she so easily own him? He had probably forfeited his man card a while ago, but somehow he didn't give two fucks. He was happy where he was. Content. Living his best life—when it wasn't somewhere freezing his balls off in the middle of a Colorado winter storm. When they uncovered their frozen bodies in the spring, he'd be wrapped around Millsy or Nelsy. Not exactly how he'd pictured himself going out. Letting down the love of his life wasn't how he had pictured his end either.

What had the bunch of them been thinking? They hadn't. A whole lot of pride and testosterone had taken the reins in this disaster. Grims blamed himself, but he hadn't twisted anyone's arm. They had gone along willingly, stupidly believing they were invincible for whatever reason, whether it was because they were professional athletes or simply because they were juveniles disguising themselves as men. Hell, even the dumbest of the dumb packed survival gear in case the worst happened. And the worst was happening all around them. They'd quickly discovered Mother Nature didn't give a shit who you were or what you owned, and she was having the last laugh.

"Imagine seeing a little Natalie running around," Nelson remarked, pulling T.J. from his dark thoughts.

T.J. grinned in spite of himself, in spite of their situation. "Don't know if I could handle a little girl." But he found himself wondering if he *could* be a good dad, maybe as a counterbalance to his own lousy upbringing.

"Girls are cool," Nelson said, and Miller quickly agreed. And he would know since he had *four* of them.

"Or a little boy you can play hockey with," Nelson added, even though his son hadn't been walking long. The guy had probably stuffed a stick in his tiny hand when he first crawled.

That picture warmed T.J. all over, which was saying something considering how fucking cold he was.

"Don't need a boy for that," Miller rejoined. "Girls play hockey too."

"True that," Nelson agreed. He coached his daughter Daisy's squirt team.

T.J. told himself that it was better he didn't have any children. It was one thing to leave behind a widow, but at least he wouldn't leave any fatherless children. Then again, he wouldn't leave *anything* of himself behind, and Natalie ... Well, she could easily find someone else who would give her those kids she wanted so badly.

Silence fell over the group, each man lost in his own thoughts. Beside T.J., Nelson seemed to doze, and T.J. was sinking into a fog of his own. In that fog skipped a carefree little girl with amber eyes that sparkled in the sun. She was in a field of golden flowers, her long chestnut hair floating behind her. It was summer, and it was warm. So warm. The girl squealed with laughter while in the background her mother laughed too. She chased the girl, swooping her up in her arms when she caught her. They dissolved in girlish giggles.

Miller's bark jolted T.J. from his reverie.

"Time to switch! Nelson, you're monkey in the middle." Had they sat there minutes or hours? T.J. wasn't sure. Hopefully, it had been hours because that meant the sun would rise soon. It had to, didn't it?

Panic swelled inside of him.

Fuck! What time is it? Can we walk out of here on frozen feet and get somewhere warm, somewhere safe, before we die from exposure?

Knock this shit off!

You need to be there for your brothers, so wake the hell up and get a goddamn grip.

"Okay, we're going to play a little game," Miller announced. "We're going to move without standing so we don't lift the emergency blanket out of place. Got it?"

With a hell of a lot of awkward maneuvering, grunting, and shuffling, they changed positions. At least it gave them something to do and brought them around, even if T.J. felt like he was pulling limbs of lead along with him. *His* limbs.

Miller had saved their asses for at least a half hour, and T.J. was motivated enough—and just clear enough—that he decided to start a conversation. Except when he began to talk, his lips were numb and his speech came out garbled, as though he were either drunk enough to blow up a breathalyzer or had spent the afternoon in the dentist's chair getting dosed with Novocain.

"What I want to know," he slurred, "is how do they that?"

"Do what?" Nelson slurred too.

"How do women curl themselves up around all our angled, awkward parts? Like, they just *mold* themselves around us. Slithering around this damn igloo with them would have been a hell of a lot easier."

"Only because it would have felt a hell of a lot better." Miller's smile came through in his voice.

"No fucking clue, but I'm fucking glad they do," Nelson added.

"Yeah, and they smell a hell of a lot better too," T.J. grumbled. "Christ, you boys smell bad!"

"You don't smell anything like vanilla and spice yourself, Shanny," Miller shot back. "And goddamn! You complain more than an old woman!"

"Why are you picking on old women?" Nelson threw in. "Do they really complain that much? I don't think so."

While Nelson droned on about the residents at his grandmother's memory care facility, T.J.'s mind wandered to hanging in the kitchen with Natalie while she baked. He was her taste tester, and damn, she made great cookies ... and cake ... and ... Fuck! Now he realized how hungry he was again.

"Fuck, I miss my wife." The quavering voice was raw, gritty, and heartbreakingly honest. T.J. was shocked when he realized it came from him.

Miller cleared his throat, and in a voice so uncharacteristically soft T.J. barely recognized it, he asked, "So what would you do if you saw her right now?"

T.J.'s mind wandered back to that beautiful little girl in the flowers, the one who was a miniature version of her mother. *I'd wrap my arms around her and bury my nose in her hair.* "Fuck, I love how her hair smells ... and feels. I'd tell her ..." He paused to mask his choking voice with a cough. "I'd tell her how much I love her." *And that she means everything to me.* Tears stung his eyes and cut tracks down his cheeks, freezing when they hit his upper lip. "That I can't wait to get her pregnant."

"Well, you just focus on that, damn it. You think about how it's going to light you up when you finally get to her, when you finally get your arms around her, you feel me?"

I need to get through this. I need to get to Natalie. "Yeah, I feel you."

Gage was tired. So damn tired. Shivering had worn him out. If he could only go to sleep, but his friends kept shaking him, jerking him back to this icy hell whenever he began to drift. And God, did he want to drift. When he drifted, he forgot about the bitter cold that ached deep down in his marrow, about the tingling and the prickling that made him itch all over. Floating, falling into sleep brought with it a euphoria that enveloped him in warmth and took away the pain. That's where he wanted to go, but his buddies wouldn't let him. At least he thought these guys were his buddies.

Why were they here? He couldn't remember.

They kept telling him to stay awake, to think about his family, his career. Did he have a family? A career? Mist swirled around a beautiful woman with a halo of blond curls. She was someone important to him, though something he'd said or done had caused her to be angry with him. What was it? What was gnawing at his soul? His muddled mind struggled to grasp it all. When someone beside him whispered the names Lily, Daisy, and Brodie, he flung himself into a mental void where he snatched at waving ribbons just out of his reach.

He pulled off his glove to scratch his face, but he couldn't feel anything—not his face, not his finger. Huh. He held his hand in front of him to inspect it, but he couldn't see it. *Too dark.* Someone crammed a glove back on that hand and shoved it into his armpit.

"Snap out of it, Nelson. You need to get through this. Your family needs you."

His family needed him. He had a family, and they needed him. The blond woman appeared again, her outline crisp this time. A pleasant, familiar scent filled his nose ... which made no sense because his noise hairs were frozen. He hoisted himself upward, and his companions pulled him back down again. A muffled voice said something about not letting him freeze to death. Was that what was happening?

His mind returned to the pretty blond lady, and contentment settled in his chest. *That's* where he wanted to be. Now she held a baby in her arms, and he wanted to hold the baby too. He wanted to wrap his arms around them both and pull them close.

Something ripped into his consciousness, blowing away some of the fog that had clouded his sluggish brain. Sharp pain accompanied a clear image of Lily holding Brodie, with Daisy beside her. Tears shimmered in her eyes, and she was begging him to come home.

"Don't leave me, Gage. Come home to us, please."

His eyes snapped open, and he felt but couldn't see someone hovering over him. The world around him was shadowed in black and shades of ultramarine. Above him, a tarp that had been flapping incessantly settled over them, quiet ripples playing across its surface. The world grew quiet, as if something had shifted in the night, and he knew he had to stay awake, no matter what. Falling asleep meant never seeing his family again, and every fiber in his being strained to see them, to hold them and tell them how much he loved them.

Don't give up on me, Lily. I'm coming home.

Chapter 13

HUDDLE AND CUDDLE, PART TWO

Quinn breathed a sigh of relief when the wind finally took a break from its whining and howling. It had been racing down his neck, working its icy fingers through every gap in his clothing for hours now, and he'd gotten over being embarrassed by his nonstop shivering long ago.

Hope lifted inside him. Maybe the wind dying down signaled rescue teams would be on the hunt for them soon. But did anyone know they were out here? Their wives knew. And though Sarah had been mad at him—and he at her—for reasons he couldn't recall, their group not returning would have triggered the women into action. Hell, they'd missed a rehearsal dinner and would soon miss Barrett's wedding.

Barrett.

He'd been moaning half the night, at first because his hip hurt like a mother. How badly had it been damaged? Who the hell knew? After it went numb with cold, though, he had switched to moaning about missing the ceremony.

"Weddings are supposed to be fun, for fuck's sake!" he had repeated at regular intervals, as though he'd been stuck on a loop. It had been funny at first but had quickly grown irritating as hell. Mercifully, he had quieted down. In fact, they were all quiet—Barrett, Grimson, and McPherson.

A voice screamed inside Quinn's muddled mind, and his heart rate kicked up. Silence was *not* a good sign.

He kicked out a sluggish foot, and it thudded against something solid. That something shifted and grunted beside him. Toeing someone on his other side, he grew alarmed when nothing moved or made noise. Quinn rolled to his side, which wasn't easy considering he was blocked in by big bodies on either side of him, one a double stack.

"What the fuck you doing?" a voice drawled.

Grimson.

"Barrett's not moving," Quinn panted.

"Because I'm lying on top of him. He *can't* move."

"Yeah, but he's not making any noise either."

Some shifting and cursing and Grims was shoving on the body beneath him. "Damn it, Barrett, you're getting married in a few hours, and I am *not* going to be the one to face Michaela and tell her I let you die on my watch." A gut-wrenching sob tore from Grimson's chest, shocking Quinn into action. Commotion on Barrett's other side announced Mac was stirring too.

Quinn yanked on Grimson's shoulder, but he flung off Quinn's hold. "He's my responsibility. I got him into this mess, and I'll get him the hell out if I have to fucking die trying."

"You're going to fucking die trying and kill him in the process too if you don't let us help," Mac said groggily. His words should have packed a wallop, but they thudded impotently against the snow cave walls of their piss-poor excuse for shelter. Not that Quinn could have constructed anything better than Shanstrom had, given their limited resources, shitty location, and even shittier weather. It was just that ... they shouldn't have been here in the first place. Though Grimson seemed eager to shoulder the burden, no one was to blame—they were *all* to blame, all having an equal share in the massive stupidity that had led them here.

By some minor miracle, only Barrett had been injured beyond bruises and scrapes. Grimson had escaped the worst of the avalanche by riding out of harm's way to the side. The only other guy astride a snowmobile had been Mac, who'd appeared to have been gobbled up by the avalanche but who had more or less ridden the avalanche down like a surfer riding a wave. Not nearly as graceful, but he'd stayed upright and survived. Unfortunately, his machine hadn't. The snowslide had churned up the sled, which had in turn taken out Barrett, who'd run after Grimson, straight across the avalanche's path. Ironically, the very object that had slammed into Barrett's hip had saved his life by landing on top of him, creating a small pocket of air that kept him from suffocating. In another twist, one of the snowmobile's skis had poked through the top layer of snow after the avalanche had settled, acting like a flag that drew them to him.

They'd all been lucky, somehow avoiding getting crushed by rolling rocks and trees, and besides Barrett, who had been fully buried, only a few had been partially covered. They'd either gotten themselves out, or, like Quinn, they'd been freed by their buddies digging them out. Stupid or not, surely the seven of them hadn't survived that disaster only to freeze to death.

Fuck dying.

His mind detoured to Sarah, as it had done most of the long night. God, he missed that sassy mouth of hers! He could picture her now, hands parked on her hips, rolling those glittering, unmatched hazel eyes of hers at him. "Sparky, that was one of the dumbest things you've ever done," she would huff. But her lips would be curled in that special telltale smile she had for only him, and she'd tease him mercilessly, not letting him take himself too seriously. No other woman on the planet would put up with his shit or even found his shit funny like she did. She'd been made just for him in every way possible. And when he thought of the way she always welcomed him into her warm body, he shuddered.

Reflexively, one of the guys pressed against him, as they'd been doing for each other all night, trying to increase their collective body heat. Barrett had gone so far as to say they should all strip down and curl up together under their mounded clothes. Quinn had written it off to delusions from the weather and his injury, though right now he would try anything if it got him home. He was even willing—*more* than willing—to welcome Sarah's mom to their home for Christmas. So what if Nola stood there scrutinizing him while he gave Sarah her Jeep? All that mattered was getting home to his wife.

Funny how banging on death's door crystallized what was important.

Dave gritted his teeth as he fought with Barrett's flopping form. He needed to get the guy moving, get blood pumping through him, needed to get him to the altar tomorrow—or was it today?

His teeth clenched a little harder when Hadley chattered out, "Do you think we'll get out of here?"

Moron! "Fuck yeah, we will. As soon as it's light, when we can see where the fuck we're going, we'll walk out. Like in the movies."

Goddamn, this was all Dave's fault. Didn't help his conscience that he'd ridden out of the avalanche virtually unscathed. *He* should have been the one lying prone, the one who'd gotten hit by the debris he'd brought down on their heads by ignoring the warnings. They wouldn't have tried high-marking without him pushing for it.

Push, push, push. That's what he did. That's what he'd been doing to Ellie, hadn't he? Hammering at her about the next kid. Jesus, Ellie! What was wrong with him? He swallowed hard to dislodge the fist crammed in his throat. *Sweetheart, I fucking love you so much. You and Kelsey both. Please forgive me for being such a goddamn dumbass.*

Fortunately—or not—Quinn's barking laugh pulled him back to their present predicament. "Well, shit! I was starting to feel good about our chances until you brought Hollywood into it."

Dave squeezed Barrett's face and rocked it side to side. "We might not make it in time for Bear's wedding—sorry, dude—but we'll get out. They'll probably be looking for us long before the sun is over the horizon." They should have found them already, but Dave had fucked up their chances when he'd led them away from where the rental company had sent them. How the hell would anyone know where to look for them?

To top it off, his snowmobile had been the only one left undamaged, and he'd hopped on it to find help ... only to get himself turned around and going in circles. By the time he figured out his mistake, he had used up nearly all the gas in his tank and had just enough to make it back to the guys.

Yeah, great leader you are, dickwad!

Beneath him, Barrett groaned, sending a thrill coursing through Dave. "That's it, dude. Stay with me. Don't go to sleep."

"Fuck, my hip!" Barrett protested weakly.

"Yeah, I know. At least you can feel it, eh? Means it's not quite as frozen as the rest of our body parts."

"Haha," Barrett chuffed, and Dave's hopes climbed a little higher. Humor was a good sign. "Fuck, I'm cold. Can't feel my feet. I *wish* I couldn't feel my damn hip."

Dave heaved him onto his side, and as he did so, his head brushed their Mylar cover, lifting it. Wind raced beneath, bringing with it a blast of arctic air.

"Shit!" Mac exclaimed.

Hadley followed this up with, "Watch the top, Grims."

"Fuck me, you're as bad as the girls!" Dave growled.

"Pretty sure the girls are a *lot* less whiny," Quinn said. "Then again, they're probably way more comfortable too."

"Considering the circumstances, I'd say we're allowed to be," Mac grumbled. "Do you think they know where we are?"

Grimson shook his head, then realized no one could see him do it. "No. But they should have called in the cavalry. They'll send up a drone. Then someone will spot our vehicles, and if they put a helo in the air—"

"Then we can all yell, 'Get to the choppa'!" Barrett coughed.

"Man, your Arnold needs some work." Ducking, Dave sat back on his haunches, though there wasn't real estate for it inside their shelter. There wasn't real estate for any actual movement. He was exhausted, but if he had his legs under him for a bit, maybe he could get feeling back into them that was more warmth than pins and needles.

"I'll work on that. Right after my wedding." Bear rolled himself into a fetal position, his knees against Mac's back. "Just want to get to my wedding and marry my woman," he whispered. "So damn lucky."

Even in the dark, Dave could feel the concerned look Hadley shot him as he patted Barrett's back. "How's that, Bear?"

Barrett seemed to choke out a sob, and Dave felt his own eyes well. "I struck gold with M. Hit the mother lode. And I don't want to give up my claim. She's the ketchup to my mustard, salt to my pepper."

Barrett might have sounded like he was hallucinating, either living out a scene from *The Treasure of the Sierra Madre* or sitting down to eat a burger at McDonald's, but Dave got it because he was one lucky fucker who had struck gold too. Like Barrett had Michaela, Dave had Ellie. She loved him in spite of his stubbornness and his jackassery; didn't matter if he deserved that love or not, she simply did. She made sure he knew it too, beyond a shadow of a doubt. And he loved her back tenfold. With her, he was the man he was meant to be. Without her, he was a shell.

As he rolled himself up into a tight ball, he blinked away tears. In his mind's eye, he saw his daughter's chubby smiling face, and he saw his wife reaching for him. And God, all he wanted in that moment was for her to take him. *Him*, not some other dude who might come after him because he was doomed to inhale his last breath here tonight, huddled on a mountain in the cold. He wasn't ready to go.

Not giving up my claim. Not yet.

"Being out here has made me realize a few things," Grimson said quietly, almost as if to himself, while he settled beside Mac.

Yeah, being on the brink of death will do that to a person, Mac wanted to say but refrained. Instead, he said, "Yeah, guess we need a natural disaster every decade or two so we can get in touch with our *feelings*, whether we want to or not."

Grimson chuckled. "Is that your way of saying we cut ourselves off from the touchy-feely stuff?"

Nah. I'm fully connected every time I'm inside Mia and I'm looking into those beautiful brown eyes.

The vision overwhelmed Mac's emotions, banding around his chest, and he choked out a cough. "Something like that."

"You getting in touch with your feelings there, Grims?" Hadley asked.

"Hard not to, don't you think? All I keep thinking about is that shit they sing in love songs about not being able to live without your one. It's true. Every last word. At least for me."

"Me too," Barrett concurred.

"What he said," Mac added.

Hadley threw in his agreement, and it struck Mac that the circumstances they found themselves in were indeed dire. Not that he hadn't thought so before, but with four of them tearing down walls and confessing matters of the heart out in the open? At the same time? It was bad, all right.

His thoughts wandered to his kids, the kids he'd planned to have with Mia, finally settling on Mia herself. Her big espresso-colored eyes, her goofy quirks and sayings, the warmth that filled her and flowed from her everywhere she went. Being with her was so damn right that the world could go to hell all around them, and as long as he had her, he was complete. Content. Rich beyond measure.

Except he didn't have her, did he? She wasn't here with him physically—*thank fuck!*—and every day he grew more uncertain that she was with him mentally. Emotionally. Where had he gone wrong that she was reluctant to marry him? Maybe she wasn't convinced he was it for her, like he was convinced she was the *only* one for him.

Sure, he looked at other women. It was as natural as breathing, though no one turned his head anymore. Picture himself with anyone but Mia? No. Fucking. Way. And the thought of not having her in his life utterly terrified him. Did the other guys feel that pull, that need, that irreplaceable connection when they thought of their women? He was pretty sure he knew the answer.

He let out a sigh.

"What's the sigh for, Mac?" Bear slurred beside him. At least the guy was talking now and again, which gave Mac hope he would make it out in one piece, if they could just hold on a little longer ... He needed to keep Bear talking.

"I was thinking—and no offense, bro—but I'd much rather cuddle with Mia than your bony ass."

Bear laughed, the sound turning to a wet chuckle rattling in his chest. "No offense taken, and right back at you. M's my favorite cuddle toy. You, not so much."

"Duly noted." Before Mac could search his fatigued brain for another topic of conversation, Hadley said, "You guys do realize Coach LeBrun will suspend us all once he finds out what we did?"

"He can't suspend us if we're dead," Grims said in a dour voice. "Well, maybe he can, but it won't affect us."

"Jesus, you're a bright ray of sunshine, Grims," Mac retorted.

"It's okay if he suspends us," Barrett chimed in. "It'll give me time for that honeymoon I had to postpone because of the season."

"Which reminds me," Hads said, "why didn't you just wait like the rest of us and get married during the off-season?"

"He wanted to strike while the iron was hot," Mac volunteered. "I get it. Gotta put a ring on that finger before the finger flies away, or some shit like that."

"Ah, a poet," Grimson chuckled. "Sounds like you might be regretting not putting a ring on it."

121

"Yeah, but it's not for lack of trying. I mean, I didn't think it was right to rush right into it the minute after I proposed. I wanted the kids to adjust."

Murmurs of approval moved through them.

And now he was spilling his guts. "I didn't figure it would drag on this long. Maybe I'm just not what she wants in a lifetime partner, and she got carried away in the moment, the grand gesture. Now that she's had time to think about it ..."

"Maybe she wants to see a more stellar saves percentage first," Hadley offered.

"Funny one, Hads." Yeah, Mac wasn't having the best start to his season, and he was a little sensitive about that too. Although, did it matter right now? Did any of it matter?

His kids mattered. Mia mattered. It mattered to him that he mattered to them. It was all he had, and if he ever got back to safety, it would be all he needed.

He sat up, accidentally bumping their Mylar cover, which set off a predictable chain reaction of grumbles from his companions. As he reached to pinch the flimsy plastic back down, something caught his eye in the gap between the snow-packed wall and the Mylar. He squinted into the darkness. Nothing. He was seeing things. Then suddenly, he glimpsed a flicker of light.

"Do they have fireflies up here?"

"In the middle of fucking winter? No!" Grimson yapped. "Now quit with the hallucinations and lie the fuck down!"

"We need your hot body." Hadley's quip came out as a sorrowful plea.

Mac waited a beat, two. *There!* The beam reappeared, and he whacked Grims's leg. "I don't think what I'm seeing is a hallucination. It could be a flashlight."

Three bodies scrambled and staggered upright, dislodging the Mylar, which remained tucked in one corner, allowing the rest to flutter in a light breeze. Mac didn't wait for the others to confirm what he'd seen. Instead he ripped off his glove, put his index finger and thumb together, pressed them to his lips, and blew.

Nothing happened. His lips were too numb. Heart racing, hope climbing a precarious cliff, he cupped his hands on either side of his mouth and shouted, "Hey! We're here!"

The Mylar cover on the other makeshift shelter rippled, and a hooded head popped out. Mac couldn't make out who the head belonged to, nor did it matter because suddenly their group was all yelling at once. The beam swung toward them but didn't reach across the dark gulf, so they continued hollering, "Over here!"

The beam split apart and spread out, becoming several beams, but they were still far away. Mac snatched the Mylar sheet and waved it in the air, and suddenly the beams converged on them, growing brighter as hulking forms loomed behind the lights.

Turned out they were headlamps.

"Is one of you Beckett Miller?" a voice boomed.

"Here," Miller rasped as he threw up his arm. The motion caused him to stagger. "How did you know?"

"Been spending a lot of time talking to your wife. She's very determined when she wants something."

Miller sank to his knees and laughed—or maybe cried, Mac couldn't tell through his own grateful tears. "And thank fuck for that."

Amen.

Chapter 14

REUNION

*V*ibrations against Paige's tummy woke her at the same time an air horn sounded. Confused, she sat up and looked around, getting her bearings. She was in the family room, where she'd dozed restlessly with the other women, sprawled in various chairs or on couches, and her phone was blaring at her. She'd set it on the loudest, most obnoxious ring she could find, coupling it with vibration mode so she didn't miss a single call.

She tossed the thing in the air as she tried to corral it, jumpy as she was with the sudden hit of adrenalin to her system. As she pressed the phone icon, she registered the others dragging themselves into sitting positions while they looked around, as befuddled as she had been seconds earlier.

"Hello?"

"Paige?" Larry Gilbert's strident voice had her coming fully alert.

Her heart leapt into her throat. "Did you find them?"

A collective gasp circled the room, and six pairs of wide eyes fixed on her. In the glow of the table lamps they had left on, she recognized dread, fear, and apprehension in their faces, and those same emotions welled up inside of her at once. As she was pulling in a steadying breath, Larry said, "I have someone who'd like to speak to you."

Before she could get out another word, a shuffling sounded, and a familiar baritone filled her with joy. "Pixie? You there?"

She clapped a hand over her mouth, and tears instantly flowed. Pulling her hand away, she cried into the phone, "Oh my God, Beck! Are you all right?"

Light flooded the room as more lamps flicked on, and the women gathered around her, pressing close. They all started buzzing at once.

"Yeah, we made it." Fatigue dragged his voice down.

She swallowed. "All of you? Is everyone okay?"

"We're okay. Some of us are a little worse for wear, but we're coming home after the paramedics are done checking us out."

Coils that had been cinched in Paige's gut gave just enough that she could catch a breath. Words broke loose, tumbling over one another. "How are you getting home? Is there somewhere where we can come get you? Are you in a hospital? How long are they keeping you? Oh God, Beck, I was so worried!"

He chuckled mildly. "We should be driving ourselves home in our own vehicles. But get ready. Barrett says he still wants the wedding to happen today."

"What?" She darted her eyes to Michaela, whose face was twisted in anguish. "But Micky sent the minister home last night. When you guys weren't back for the rehearsal din—"

"Well, call the guy back. Although Bear says he'd prefer the wedding be a little later. I think the plan was for two before, so maybe we push it to four?"

She tried not to focus on the absurdity of going from devastation to discussing a delayed wedding. "The minister is a she, but either way, I think it's too late."

Justin, dressed in his crisp blacks as though he'd just starched himself all over, stepped forward and held up his finger. "If you're looking for a minister, I'm self-ordained, and I'd be happy to do the honors, assuming the paperwork is in order."

Michaela's face brightened like an LED light at the highest setting, and she clapped her hands together. "Oh yes! Please! I have everything!"

"Beck, we're a go!" Paige shouted.

"Fantastic! I'll let Bear know. I gotta go now. Search and Rescue wants their phone back."

"Beck!"

"Yeah, pixie?"

"Everything I said before ... when we argued ..."

"We argued? Funny, I don't remember that. All I remember is how much I love you."

Her heart expanded several sizes and oozed like a heated Brie. "I love you too," she whispered.

"You can show me later."

He ended the call, and Paige leapt up from the couch and filled everyone in. Happy chatter filled the room. "Oh my gosh, we have a wedding to get ready for. There's so much to do!"

"No, we were already ready," Natalie pointed out as she bounced on her toes.

"We just need to move a few things and get cleaned up," said Lily, her eyes dancing with happiness.

The room was abuzz with excited feminine voices. It gave Paige's heart a helium boost.

"When will the guys be here?" Ellie asked.

Paige said, "I don't know. Paramedics are checking them out. What time is it now?"

"Five thirty," Sarah announced.

Justin cleared his throat. "They're going to be hungry when they get here. I'll get started on breakfast."

A scream-fest ensued, reminding Paige of tween sleepovers from her past, but the giddiness had nothing to do with Justin's breakfast. In fact, Paige wouldn't have been able to choke down a forkful of anything at that moment, and she was sure she wasn't alone. After hours suspended in a twilight where they didn't know how to find their men or if they were alive, the atmosphere transformed from silent anguish to one akin to children tearing apart presents on Christmas morning. So much joy!

While Justin's waitstaff scattered to prepare for the wedding, the women scurried to their rooms to prepare for the homecoming. After showering and styling her hair loose, just the way Beckett liked it, Paige shimmied into a bra-and-panties set he had bought her, a pair of skinny jeans, pointy-heeled booties, and a form-fitting beaded ivory sweater that was one of his favorites because it showed off a little cleavage. To heck with the baby fat. Her wardrobe selection wasn't about hiding it; it was about pleasing him.

When she emerged and looked around, she realized each one of them had done the exact same thing. They were a group of seven stunners, if she did say so herself, and they waited in nervous anticipation for the vehicles that would bring their husbands and fiancés home. Crowding the windows in the foyer, they arranged each other's hair, fixed a button, or straightened a collar while their eyes remained glued to the winding pathway.

When Paige spotted the first set of headlights bouncing up the driveway and recognized Gage's Range Rover, her heart jackhammered in her chest. All thought of perfectly brushed hair or neatly smoothed clothing flew from her mind as she raced out the front door with the others. They arrayed themselves in a comical but unintentional line, like middle schoolers in PE during the dreaded dance segment, and Paige bobbed on the balls of her feet. The other women bounced too, emitting little squeaks and giggles.

The Range Rover sped into the parking area, followed closely by Quinn's truck, sliding to a diagonal stop that spat gravel in different directions. Some of the women ducked, laughing, arms over their heads to avoid being hit by the ricocheting rocks. The truck came to rest perpendicular to the SUV, followed by Dave's truck, trailered snowmobile in tow. Though he didn't come in quite as hot as Gage and Quinn had, he didn't bother with any kind of parking decorum, and the truck sprawled across the parking area where he left it after killing the engine.

Doors flew open at once, and T.J., the first man to step out, let out a war whoop and held his arms wide, his head on a swivel until his eyes landed on Natalie running at him. Quinn nearly fell on his way out of his truck but straightened in time to catch

Sarah as she sprinted full-out into his arms. Gage barely killed the engine before Lily was at his side and he was lifting her into the air, his smile challenging the brightness of the morning sun. Mac bellowed Mia's name as he loped toward her, and she answered with a scream of "Mac!" in return.

Beckett finally stumbled from the SUV, his shimmering eyes fixed on Paige. He started to move, but she reached him before he had put much space between himself and the vehicle. She was on him—literally—jumping him and wrapping her legs around his waist like a monkey climbing a tree. His arms banded around her, and he buried his face in her neck, breathing, "Andie," and, "Thank God," over and over. She pulled back to run her hands over his wind-burned face.

"I look pretty bad, huh?" he murmured. "And probably smell worse."

Tears streaming down her face, she shook her head. "No. You're the most beautiful man I've ever seen."

He chuckled. "You need glasses, pixie." Then his fingers wound in her hair, and he pulled her to him before crashing his mouth down on hers, stealing the breath from her lungs as he kissed her long, hard, and deep.

Her ankles were still locked at his back when he uncoupled his mouth from hers. "Am I too heavy?" She began to squirm, but he held her fast, tears filling his beautiful blue eyes. He leaned his forehead against hers.

"No, stay exactly where you are."

"I thought I'd lost you," she cried softly. "But you're okay? You're not hurt?"

"I'm okay. Just tired and hungry." He glanced over his shoulder. "I should help Grimson."

Paige slid from Beckett, reluctantly releasing his neck, and realized Dave was helping Blake from the truck. Beside him stood Ellie, a concerned frown on her face and her hand covering her mouth, and Michaela, who alternately wrung her hands and swiped at her leaky eyes.

"What happened to Blake?" Paige followed Beckett around the hood of the truck.

Blake wrenched his eyes from Michaela and grinned at Paige. "Took a snowmobile to the hip."

"Do you need a doctor? Can you walk?" Michaela cried.

Blake shook off Dave's hold and limped toward her, a tender look on his face.

"Nah, he's a tough guy," someone yelled—Mac, Paige thought.

Blake wrapped his arms around Michaela, who slid her hands around his shoulders while she obviously tried not to sob. "The paramedics who checked me out gave me an all-clear," he said. "I'll follow up with the team doctor when I get back. I can't walk fast, but I sure as hell can stand up in front of a minister today. You still willing to marry the only dumbass who got hurt, Curly?"

Paige sank against Beckett's side, fighting tears of her own, and he curled his arm around her and snugged her against his side.

Michaela nodded at Blake and choked out, "Wouldn't want to disappoint all our guests."

"No, we certainly wouldn't want to do that." Then he kissed her as though they didn't have an audience.

Beckett tugged Paige toward the house. "C'mon. I could use a shower and a nap."

As he opened the front door for her, she looked up at him and smirked. "What kind of nap?"

"Not a noisy nap, if that's what's running through your dirty little mind, which I love, by the way. I'm talking about a real nap—and a pile of food—so I can deliver on the noisy part later." He waggled his eyebrows at her.

Can't wait.

Natalie sat at the kitchen table, elbow propped and head cradled in her palm as she stared at T.J. wolfing down a plate heaped with scrambled eggs, three kinds of meat, and a stack of waffles.

Her man was hungry, and she tried to keep the moony teenager look from overtaking her face as she watched him eat. She couldn't hold back the little sigh that escaped her, though. Disheveled as he was from his night in the wild, the man was still gorgeous, and she couldn't get enough of watching him.

Around the massive table, a similar scene played out among the clustered couples. Conversation had bounced from man to man as he described the ordeal from his perspective, but now it had subsided to private talk between each man and woman.

Dear God!

Natalie shuddered at how close she'd come to losing T.J. A sob bubbled in her throat, followed by the familiar prick of tears in her eyes. Seeming to sense her jangled emotions, he took one of her hands in his, kissed it, and dropped it on his thigh.

Playfully, she shoved a bowl of fresh berries toward him, and he shoved it back with a wink.

"Nice try there, Amber Eyes, but the healthy stuff is going to wait." He pointed at the bowl with his fork. "Why don't you eat it?"

She shook her head. She hadn't been able to eat since they'd received the terrible news last night, and she wasn't sure when her stomach would allow food to pass.

He paused his eating and leaned in conspiratorially. "What we argued about the other day on our way up here ..."

She straightened. "Should we talk about this later?" she whispered.

"I have something I want to say to you, Nat."

"It doesn't matter," she hurried. "I had lots of time to think about it, and I'm willing to—"

"No." His hazel eyes shimmered with tears, and her heart went into a gallop. He covered her hand, still resting on his lap. "I had a lot of time to think too," he murmured, "and I realized ..." He swallowed, his Adam's apple bobbing in his powerful neck. "I don't know why I've been such a dick about it, but I do know I don't want to wait, Nat. I want to start our family. Now."

She must have looked all kinds of shocked because he added, "It's amazing how clear things become when you think you might not make it." He nodded as if to make his point, then returned to his plate and made short work of his waffles.

"Say something," he mumbled around his food.

"I-I don't know what to say," she stammered. She placed her fingertips against his forehead. "You sure you didn't crack your skull on a snowmobile?"

"I'm sure," he laughed. "Too hardheaded, remember?"

She nodded and pressed her knuckles in her eyes to keep more tears from falling. God, she was a blubbering mess! He shot her an achingly tender look. "I'm sorry, sweetheart. Sorry it took me so long. Are we good?"

Without a thought for the people sitting around the table, she threw her arms around his neck, whispering, "Always."

He dragged her close and buried his nose in her hair. "Christ, I love you, Nat. So fucking much."

Before she could regain her voice and tell him she loved him right back, a throat clear pulled them apart. "Maybe take it to your room, huh? People are still eating here," Gage teased.

Ignoring Gage, T.J. looked deep in her eyes. "What a great idea." He rose and held out his hand to her. "What do you say, Mrs. Shanstrom?"

She placed her hand in his and let him pull her up. "I say lead the way, Mr. Shanstrom."

He stepped from the table, paused, and looked in different directions before giving her a sheepish look. "*You'll* have to lead the way. I don't know where our room is."

With a laugh, she pulled him after her, nearly floating above the floor.

Gage's eyes followed T.J. and Natalie out of the room. With a grin, he looked back at Lily. "I could use a lie-down myself. What do you say? Join me?"

Butterflies erupted in her tummy, as they had been doing sporadically since she'd set eyes on her husband climbing out of his Range Rover. God, she loved this man! "Sounds good. Not sure I can sleep, though."

He laced his fingers with hers, and his grin turned downright cocky. He leaned in and kissed her temple, dropping his voice low. "Is that your way of seducing me?"

She let out a laugh and shoved at him with her free hand. "No. I was just warning you because my being in the room might disturb you."

"You being in the same room never disturbs me. Besides, right now I can sleep enough for both of us." He released her hand and tucked a strand of hair behind her ear. She leaned into his warm touch, and he cupped her cheek. "I just want to hold you next to me," he murmured. "I want to know you're there. After last night, I really need that, Lil. I need *you*."

Without her permission, her eyes welled up and tears spilled down her cheeks. "Then you have me," she whispered.

They ambled back to their bedroom hand in hand. His eyes widened when she opened the door and he took in the space. "Wow! If I'd known this is where you were sleeping the other night, I would have crashed here, invited or not."

"Pretty sweet, huh?"

He wrapped his arms around her waist. "Yes, she certainly is." Lily felt a blush heat her cheeks as Gage pulled her toward the bed. Dropping on the edge of the mattress, he shucked his shoes, tugged off his sweater, and lay back, flopping his arms wide. He patted the bed beside him. "Come lie down."

She kicked off her own shoes and stretched out beside him, smoothing his T-shirt over his chiseled abdomen and chest. Gathering her close, he rested his chin on the crown of her head. "I must smell awful, but if I try to get cleaned up right now, I might fall asleep in the shower. Do you mind too much?"

She snuggled closer and sniffed his stubbly neck. "You don't smell awful. You smell like you, for which I am extremely grateful." *I almost lost you.* Breath caught in her throat.

He chuckled, and his breath ruffled her hair. "Well, *you* smell really, really good."

Settling her cheek on his chest, she reveled in the sound of his heart beating strong and steady. Maybe she *could* fall asleep, lulled as she was by the rhythm.

"Lil." His voice rumbled through his chest.

"Yes?"

"I, ah, I just wanted to say I was way off base about my mom the other day."

She craned her neck to look at him and placed her finger against his lips. "Shh. We can talk later."

"No, I need to say this now." He stared into her eyes for a beat, and she could have sworn he looked into the depths of her soul and saw everything there. He had a way of doing that. "I'm so sorry I didn't stick up for you. I've been trying to walk both sides of the line, and I made you feel like you're not as important as my mom. Nothing could be farther from the truth. *You* are my world. You and Daisy and Brodie."

"I know that. And I know how hard you try to please us both. I shouldn't have pushed."

One corner of his mouth tipped up. "Don't tell my mom, but while we were freezing to death out there, all I could think about was you—you and the kids. My mom entered my thoughts sometime later, but only in a vague 'This is going to suck for her' sort of way. I guess that makes me a bad son. But when I thought about you ..." His eyes filled with tears, making hers rim again. He pushed her hair from her forehead and in a halting voice said, "You're my heart, Lily. I'd be lost without you."

"And I'd be lost without you. So lost. I've always known that, but when you were out there and I didn't know if you were ..." She choked out a sob.

He gently pushed her head back to his chest. "Shh. Everything worked out, and we're okay." She relaxed against his warmth, his strength, and just when she thought he'd drifted off, he said, "And for the record, I don't think you spend too much. I love that you take pride in our home and our family. Besides, we can afford it."

Hoisting herself on an elbow, she searched his face. "Can we? Are you worried about getting traded or sent down?"

He blinked. "It's crossed my mind, but it's not our finances I'm worried about."

"You hide it well, Professor. I didn't know."

"I didn't want to worry you."

"What worries me is you shouldering the load alone. You can lean on me, you know. I love you no matter what, and I won't break under the pressure. I *want* to be there for you. I promised to love you for better or for worse, and I meant every word."

He caressed her cheek with the back of his finger. "What if I get traded? Or no one signs me when my contract's up?"

She shrugged. "I don't know. After witnessing your *Fast and Furious* driving moves today, I think you have a future as a stunt driver."

"What can I say? I was motivated," he laughed. A breath later, he continued. "Seriously, Lil, what do you think?"

"Other families figure these things out. So will we. Hockey isn't forever." She drew in a sharp breath when she realized what she'd said. "Does that bother you? To know it won't go on forever?"

He shook his head. "No. I love the game, but that didn't enter my mind either while I was out there. So I'd say I have everything I need for a happily-ever-after right here." He frowned. "Well, I might be missing one thing."

"What's that?"

"Sing to me. I think I'd like to hear 'Amazing Grace.'"

As she'd done so many times before, she sang for him, pouring her soul into the words. And as he drifted off, peaceful in her arms, she sent a thank-you heavenward.

Chapter 15

WE GO TOGETHER LIKE EGGS AND BACON

The kitchen table emptied as more couples drifted off to their rooms, but Quinn wasn't done eating. In fact, he was halfway through his third helping, and Sarah was pretty sure Justin was ready with the fourth if Quinn called for it.

"Filling up yet, Sparky?" She couldn't hide her amusement. She was giddy simply sitting next to him and couldn't keep from touching his shoulder, his leg, his hair. He was real. Solid. Alive.

His mouth lifted in a lazy smile. "Hold on to your panties, Sunshine. Almost done. Then I'm all yours. Know what you're going to do with me yet?"

"Ah, yeah. I'm sending you straight to the shower, then putting you to bed—alone—so you're ready in time for the wedding that's taking place"—she glanced at the microwave clock— "in five hours."

Quinn swiped a napkin across his mouth. "Well, that's disappointing." He flashed her a grin that popped his dimples.

"You can't be serious," she scoffed. "You have to be completely exhausted."

He nodded. "Yeah, but I heard this rumor about you skinny-dipping in the hot tub, and I needed to focus on something to keep me going up there so I wouldn't freeze to death."

"So *that's* what you thought about?"

"Naturally. And now the picture is stuck in my head, and it's messing with me. Big-time." He glanced down at himself, and his grin broadened.

She rolled her eyes, stifling a laugh. "Wow. Apparently, even a brush with death can't cool Quinn Hadley's libido."

His expression softened, and so did his voice. He leaned in to steal a kiss. "Seriously, I thought about you. A lot. About us. And not necessarily naked in a hot tub, though I'd be lying if I said my mind didn't wander there a few times." He took her hands in his. "Let's go someplace where we can be alone."

She led him toward their bedroom, but he stopped her when they passed a library tucked into a corner of the castle. He flicked his finger toward a love seat. "This looks like a good place."

She frowned. "For what?"

"For me to tell you a few things. If you take me anywhere near a bed or a hot tub, I won't have enough brain function to talk, let alone say what I have to say."

"This sounds serious."

They sank onto the love seat together, knee to knee, her hands cradled in his. He canted his head and looked at her with those soulful brown eyes of his. "When I was stuck up there and didn't know if we'd make it back, I realized how much you mean to me." He placed one of her hands against his heart, covering it with his, and she nearly lost it. "I love you so fucking much. You know that, right?" His eyes glossed over. She nodded, words trapped in her throat. He heaved out a sigh. "I also realized how petty I was when I got pissed off about your mom maybe spending Christmas with us."

Shaking her head, she slid her hands from his and squeezed his lips shut.

His eyebrows climbed his forehead. "Mmph?" When she loosened her hold, he said, "Trying to apologize here."

She clasped his hands between hers. "I know, and I want you to stop because you don't owe me an apology. *I* owe *you* one. You want to start our own tradition, and that's so ... so sweet." Tears pricked her eyes, but she didn't care. Let him see her cry. Almost losing him had made her realize she wasn't the tough girl she pretended to be, and she was okay with that discovery. "After I had time to think about it, I was so touched. I mean, how lucky can a girl be? Her husband wants to spend Christmas with only her." She searched his face, but his expression was blank, his jaw slack. "I didn't appreciate the gesture for what it was. Instead, I sort of shit all over your plans. I'm so sorry, Quinn." She offered him a contrite smile. "I love you, you know. A hell of a lot, and not just because of that."

He blinked and jerked his head as if someone had snapped him back to the present. "So does this mean—"

"Christmas will be just us." Any qualms Sarah had about breaking the news to her mother were crushed when Quinn's face lit up like one of the Christmas trees decorating the castle.

"Sweet!" He laughed, and her heart lifted several inches. "This will be the best Christmas ever!"

She barreled ahead. "Are we done here?"

"Uh, yeah?"

"Good. Let's get you to bed."

"How about a dip in one of the hot tubs first? Just us. Clothing optional." His smile turned wicked. "*That's* one of the reasons you love me a helluva lot, isn't it? Admit it."

"You're incorrigible."

"And you love it," he said smugly.

"Yeah, I do."

Dave pushed his plate away and patted his ridiculously flat belly. "I'm not sure if that was one of the best breakfasts I've ever had because I was starving or if it was one of the best breakfasts I've ever had, period."

Seated beside him, Ellie grinned at him and ran her fingertips across his broad back. "Better now?"

"Not quite." He curled an arm around her and dragged her onto his lap, pulling her close. He laid his head on her shoulder and seemed to breathe her in. "Jesus, you smell so damn good. And you feel even better."

They sat like that for long minutes until he shifted her bottom so she faced him, straddling him. She snaked her arms around his neck, a little self-conscious. They weren't alone. He tucked her hair behind her ear, touching it reverently.

"Better now," he murmured. His eyes dropped to her mouth before lifting slowly back up again, as if he was memorizing her face. "Hey, gorgeous," he whispered.

"Hey, handsome."

A throat cleared beside them, and she nearly vaulted off Dave's lap. "Beg pardon," Justin said as he picked up Dave's plate, "but are you done with your meal?"

Dave nodded. "Yes, thanks. Two helpings were plenty. That was fantastic."

"Glad it hit the spot."

Ellie watched Justin's retreat over her shoulder, settling back into Dave when the chef was out of sight, though she was hyper-aware that others bustled nearby.

Dave stroked her cheek with his thumb. "Why are you blushing?"

"Not used to the PDA, I guess." She squirmed in his lap.

He cupped her nape and drew her close. "Well, get used to it."

"Dave," she giggled right before he kissed her ... and kissed her ... and kissed her.

Part of her wanted to pull away, but a different part—the side that won out—melted into the kiss, melted into him. God, the man knew how to move his mouth! When he broke the kiss, she gasped for air.

One corner of his mouth quirked. "Been thinking about that ever since I got us all stuck on that damn mountain. Just needed to say hello to my girl."

"Well, hello to you too. You certainly know how to take a girl's breath away."

He kissed her again. "Only one girl whose breath I want to steal." She wriggled again, preparing to vacate, but he tightened his hold. "Where are you going?"

"Um, maybe we should move someplace more ... private?"

"Why? It's good for people to see a man loving on his wife."

"Yes, but ..."

Something like recognition passed through his eyes. "Damn, I'm doing it again."

She cinched her brows together. "Doing what?"

Swiftly but gently, he moved her back into her own chair, confusing the hell out of her. That bewilderment must have shown. He leaned in, his arm draped across the back of her chair, a look of anguish plastered on his face. "Being pushy. It's what I do. Like a bull. I push and push until I get my way or break something. It's why we got stranded. I almost killed us." Straightening, he shook his head. "I'm sorry if I made you uncomfortable just then. I wasn't thinking ... something I've realized I do often."

"What, not thinking?" she blurted.

"Yeah. I just ... do shit, say shit, without thinking it through. Like I said, I push."

"Not true. The Dave I know is very deliberate."

"The Dave you know," he chuffed in disgust. He regarded her for a long beat. "What the hell do you see in me anyway?"

She gawked at him. *What?*

He rubbed the back of his neck and blew out a breath. "When I look at you, I think 'How did I get so fucking lucky? I don't deserve her. She's beautiful, she's smart, she's successful. What the hell does she see in a dumbass jock like me?' All I'm good for is playing hockey, and pretty soon I won't even be good for that." His hazel eyes drilled into hers.

Whoa. She slipped back into his lap and looped her arms around his neck again, searching his eyes for a clue. "What's going on here, Dave?"

He looked as though he was on the verge of divulging something, but then his eyes shuttered. He wrapped his arms around her, drew her close, and buried his face in her neck. His voice quaked. "I just want to hold you, El. Hold you until I know you're real."

She hugged him tightly to her. "I'm real, Dave. I'm not going anywhere."

Catching her off guard, he cried softly against her shoulder, and she quelled the alarms going off in her head. Dave was the most stoic man she knew, and while he harbored plenty of emotions, he normally kept them locked up.

He seemed to pull himself together, and she whispered, "I think a few hours of sleep would do us both a world of good."

Without protest, he let her lead him to the bedroom, where he lay down on the bed. She wrapped herself around him, her front to his back, cocooning his big frame as best she could. *Thank God you came back to me.*

But had he?

Freshly showered, Mac perched at the edge of the bed in boxer briefs and one of Mia's favorite T-shirts. The same blue as his eyes, it was worn down to a softness that called to her to touch. It didn't hurt that the fabric skimmed those hard planes and angles she loved to feel beneath her hands.

They had just hung up from talking to his kids, Mason and Riley, because he had needed to hear their voices. Nothing was said about the last twenty-four hours, and she sensed he was grappling with beasts in his mind, looking for connections to tether him to *this* reality.

She wasn't sure she understood it fully, but she didn't need to. Whatever he needed, she was willing to give him.

She threw her arm around his big shoulders and leaned her head against him. "I'm so glad Blake and Michaela get to have their wedding today after all. Is he hurt bad?"

"I don't know," Mac sighed. "It was my snowmobile that hit him, did you know that?"

"But I thought you rode out the avalanche."

"I *did*, but the sled got away from me and ended up taking him out." He shook his head. "Fuck! What if I ended his career?"

She bit back the playful scoff in her throat when she saw the devastation on his handsome face. How could he possibly think Blake getting hurt was *his* fault? "Mac, even if it turns out his career is done because of the injury, how is it your fault? I mean, you're blaming yourself for something that was clearly out of your control. Can we focus instead on the fact that despite the odds, you all *survived*? Not to mention, it's a miracle you stayed on top! You could have gotten tangled up and rolled down the mountain, getting smashed against rocks and trees all the way down until you were nothing but a bloody pulp." Her voice became a squeak as tears choked her. "I'd be identifying your mangled corpse right now instead of sitting next to you."

He craned his head and looked down at her, amusement dancing in his eyes. "Kind of a gruesome description, don't you think?" He exaggerated a flinch.

"That's my point. It could have been gruesome, but it turned out not to be. Your guardian angels were working overtime— even Blake's. Your sled could have killed him, but it didn't. And here you are, in one whole piece, and thank God!" She threw her arms around him and cried against his chest, soaking her favorite T-shirt.

"Hey, hey," he chuckled against her hair as his arms wound around her. "Okay. I get your point. Now will you please stop crying? You know I can't take it."

"Wuss-bag." Her voice was muffled against him.

He rubbed her back in slow circles. "Yeah, when it comes to you, I admit it. I'm a *total* wuss-bag." He tilted her chin up with his fingers. "I'm okay. Now stop."

"Don't ever do that again."

He pushed her hair out of her eyes. "What? Admit I'm a wuss-bag?"

"No, go snowmobiling."

"Can't promise that."

"Okay. No high-marking, then."

"I'll take it under consideration."

"You're impossible."

"I know." He gave her a cockeyed grin. "It's part of my charm."

"Marry me, Mac."

His jaw dropped open—not the reaction she had hoped for—then he narrowed his baby blues. "When?"

An idea struck like lightning. "Today, when Blake and Michaela tie the knot. The guy can marry us too. We'll make it a double wedding!" Now she was half crying, half babbling, and utterly insane. Such an attractive combination; she was pleasantly surprised when he didn't run for the door.

Instead, a laugh rumbled through his chest. When she didn't laugh too, he gaped at her. "You're serious, aren't you?"

She sniffled and bobbed her head. "I had a lot of time to think, and more than anything, I want to be married to you and for us to be a family. If something were to happen to you, I want your kids to have a mom in place." They had talked about her adopting the kids from the very beginning, and she'd always been willing, but never had she imagined Mac not being there. Now she could, and she didn't want the kids to be alone.

When he said nothing, she prodded. "I thought you were ready. Do you need more time to figure out if you want to marry me?" She'd been teasing, but suddenly she was trying to find purchase in quicksand. His desire to marry her had been unwavering, but what if, after being around her crazy all these months—

"Christ on a cracker!" He exploded in a mirthless laugh. "I asked! And in a damn spectacular way, if I do say so myself. Who does that if they're not sure they want to marry the person? And remember, you accepted." He wagged a finger in her face before cupping it in his big hands. "I don't need more time to know what I already know, what I've always known. I want you in my life, Mia. And if that means I have to wait ten years before you'll finally say 'I do' in front of a preacher, then I'll wait. I don't have much choice. There's no one else for me."

Once more, she threw her arms around him and cried against his poor shirt. "I love you."

Gently, he grasped her upper arms, slid them from his body, and held her apart. He canted his head and delved into her eyes. "These past twenty-four hours really had an effect on me, but I didn't realize they had one on you too. I'm sorry."

And that, right there, was one of the many reasons she was crazy about this man. Despite her nutso behavior, and though he'd endured a harrowing ordeal, he was able to put himself in her shoes and understand what the nightmare had been like for her. Almost losing him had sent her tumbling over a virtual ledge of her own.

She hiccupped. "I'm sorry for being so ridiculous."

"Why are you calling my girl ridiculous?" he asked softly.

"Because I'm crying and carrying on, and *you're* the one who nearly died."

"By getting my body mangled," he said dryly. He pulled her to him, cradling her in his arms. "You're not ridiculous. And your 'crying and carrying on' feels pretty damn good. It means you care what happens to me. I love that," he murmured. "I love *you*."

She wriggled free of his hold. "So you'll marry me?"

He leveled his gaze on her. "Absolutely. But not today."

She blinked at him.

"Mia," he reasoned, "I want our families and friends there. I want the kids to be part of the ceremony. Riley would never forgive us if she didn't get to be the flower girl."

Oh, he had a point there.

He pressed a knuckle under her chin and lifted her head a little higher. "And honestly, I don't think Blake and Michaela would appreciate us horning in on their special day. So what do you say we pick a date in July—that's only seven months away—and we start planning now. That way everyone can come, including the guys from my team, *and*"—he swiped at fresh tears on her cheeks—"a July wedding gives us time for a real honeymoon." He gave her a familiar eyebrow waggle.

"Oh. Yes, please."

"Come on, Loops. What do you say? Pull up your calendar and let's lock down the date."

"Mac?"

"Hmm?"

"I love you."

"I know."

Chapter 16

TILL DEATH DO US PART

Mac looked on as Grimson brushed a piece of lint from Barrett's suit, then squared up his coat.

Barrett grinned, his face filled with glee. "You gonna straighten my tie too, Dad? Slide me a few extra bucks for prom night?"

Grimson shoved his shoulder. "Fuck you, asshole. Just trying to make sure your looks don't scare the shit out of your bride and send her screaming. This is the thanks I get?"

Barrett looked down at himself. "What's wrong with how I look?"

"Besides your face, you mean?" quipped Owen Ferguson, Barrett's best friend and best man.

The boys were gathered in a butler's pantry. It adjoined the formal dining room, which had been transformed for the wedding with swaggy evergreen shit and tons of twinkly lights above a little platform. *A little overkill*, thought Mac, but the girls had oohed and aahed over it, calling it a mountain-elegant wedding chapel. It did have a nice view, overlooking a snow-covered meadow. As for Barrett, Mac doubted the dude would notice his surroundings. He was too nervous, and all he could talk about was seeing Michaela a few minutes from now. Mac got it; he could already feel butterflies in his own stomach, and he was seven months away from being in Barrett's perfectly polished black shoes.

Someone had poured shots of bourbon, and Mac handed Barrett one. "You sure you're ready for this?"

Barrett laughed. "For what, the shot?"

Mac held up his shot glass and grinned. "No, dumbass. The wedding. Or, more precisely, the wedding night. With that hip of yours, I'd say any Michael Jackson moves are out."

"Nah, I got this. I'm just going to lie back and let *her* do all the work. Love me some cowgirl." A salacious grin split Bear's face from ear to ear, and Mac had to lock out the visual of a naked Mia playing cowgirl on *him* or risk the appearance of a blatant boner at a wholly inappropriate time. Wait. Was there ever an appropriate time for a boner to break out? Well, yeah, but not in the company of his bros. No, that was best kept behind closed doors, and he planned on some of that action post-wedding with Mia in the privacy of their bedroom.

The boys toasted the groom and downed their drinks, and Justin, the chef slash minister, stuck his head in. "Ready when you are."

Guys teased Barrett good-naturedly as he pulled in and pushed out a few breaths. "Let's do this." He limped through the doorway, and they trailed him into the dining room, back-slapping and chuckling.

Soon Mac's friend and teammate stood beside Michaela, dressed in white and as radiant as a Christmas bride should be. Facing Justin on his preacher platform, they repeated their vows, and Mac took in the moving scene with keen interest. Flanking Blake was Ferguson, while Paige Miller stood beside Michaela. Beckett beamed at his wife like an utter goofball, not that Mac blamed him. He was having trouble corralling the unstoppable smile he had every time he looked down at Mia by his side. She was—no offense to the bride—by the far the most gorgeous woman in the room, in a red dress that molded to her perfect curves and high heels that accentuated her lean, shapely calves.

He leaned down, pulling in her flowery fragrance, and whispered, "This will be us soon."

She turned her head, her brown eyes shimmering and her smile wide. "July fourteenth. Can't wait."

"I love you," he mouthed.

Giving him a saucy wink, she mouthed back, "I know."

He stifled a laugh and pulled her against him, dropping a kiss on her head as she relaxed into him.

Yep, this was shaping up to be the best Christmas ever. He was one lucky son of a bitch.

Quinn studied the room while the minister—or was he the chef?—droned on, reading from a book he held in his hands. Had his and Sarah's wedding been this long? He had no idea because he'd been so damn twitchy he couldn't remember a thing except the last bit, where he got to kiss her. By far, that had been his favorite part of the ceremony. Ask any married guy here, and he'd agree.

Since there were no chairs in the room, everyone stood. Sarah was close beside him, tugging on his hand as his eyes took a tour of the decorations livening up the room. He leaned down, offering her his ear. "You're not paying attention," she whispered.

"It's taking forever," he replied.

"It's only been five minutes!" She drew back and gave him a play glare, which was when he noticed tears glistening in her eyes.

Something in his chest shifted with the realization that his little Miss Sassy Sunshine was getting all choked up. Rarely did she show her sentimental side. He squeezed her hand. She squeezed his back, hard, and he settled into listening as Blake and Michaela pledged themselves to one another. Simple words, yet powerful. The two looked at each other as if no one else in that room existed. Quinn got a little choked up himself.

Finally came the part where Barrett got the nod to kiss Michaela, and Quinn huffed, "Finally!"

Sarah grinned up at him. "You have no patience, Sparky."

Amid the expected clapping and wolf whistles, the guy actually dipped his bride, bad hip and all. "Way to go, Bear!" Quinn whooped. Then he dropped his mouth to Sarah's ear. "Wrong. I have a *lot* of patience ... when it counts." Pulling back, he wiggled his eyebrows at her.

With a nod from Grimson, the boys gathered up hockey sticks they'd stashed earlier and formed two lines opposite one another, like a gauntlet. They crossed their sticks in the air, and Barrett led Michaela beneath the arch while the entire group cheered. Once bride and groom passed through, the guys beat their sticks on the floor in a hockey salute of approval, then smacked their sticks together. Grimson gave them all the stink-eye—his silent command to put the sticks away. Yeah, alcohol, a party, and hockey sticks. Not a safe combination.

As people filed out after the happy couple, Quinn leaned his stick in a corner. Sarah cocked her head at him. "What made you so fidgety during the ceremony anyway?"

You. He glanced around the space and shrugged. "I was just admiring the extra touches. The lights."

She blinked in surprise. "Really? Since when are you a decorator?"

"Do you not remember our first date?" He jabbed his thumbs against his chest. "Let me remind you, I am *Mr.* Twinkle Lights."

Sarah started laughing and didn't stop.

"Wow. Talk about spearing a guy's ego."

"Okay. You did a wonderful job stringing lights for our first date. In fact, I still get misty-eyed when I remember it." She paused to dab at the corners of her eyes.

He wrapped an arm around her shoulders and pulled her against him. "Aw, Sunshine. Was it that bad?"

She shook her head against his chest. "No, you big oaf. It was wonderful." Looking up at him, she parked her chin on his chest. Her eyelashes were clumped together like star points, which only added to the glitter in their hazel depths. "So wonderful, in fact, that you get to decorate our entire house as soon as we get home. A great start to our Christmas tradition."

He opened and closed his mouth.

She grinned. "I'll help."

"Help distract me, that's what you'll do. Something you're really good at." He leaned down and stole a kiss.

"I do my best. Shall we join the party?"

"Yeah, but we're leaving early."

"Leaving for where?"

"The other wing, where our bedroom is."

She gave him a wickedly seductive smile. "You're on, Sparky."

"They look so happy!" Ellie gushed from the side of the big-ass family room—at least Dave thought it was a family room rather than a concert hall—where they stood sipping champagne and nibbling hors d'oeuvres. Well, Ellie nibbled while Dave chomped.

She peeped up at him, her slate-blue eyes shifting hue with every change in her expression. Had they always done that? He swallowed.

"So what about us? Are we happy?" she asked softly.

Her question rocked him like a blindside hit on the ice. "What? Why would you ask that? Are you telling me we're *not* happy?" Panic welled inside him, and he pulled her into a quiet corner. "Is this why you want to hold off on having another baby? You're thinking of ... of leaving?"

Her eyes went as wide as the hors d'oeuvres plate in her hand. "No, Dave! I just meant you're so stoic, and I can't always read you, and sometimes I wonder about us, especially lately because ..." She gulped, and his stomach twisted into knots, prepared to eject the food he'd just consumed. Sadness reflected in her big eyes, and her voice dropped to a whisper. "Because I've been so reluctant to, um, get pregnant."

Now *his* eyes bulged. "Jesus, El. You should never have to wonder how I feel about you, and the fact that you do means I've done a lousy job letting you know." His hand found hers, and he traced a line from her knuckles to her wrist and back again. "Ellie," he sighed, his eyes riveted to hers, "I think about you all. The. Fucking. Time. And I'm not talking about sex." He paused to wag his head. "Okay. If I'm being totally honest, I think about being *with* you a hell of a lot while I'm thinking about you." For a guy in his mid-thirties, it surprised him how much his body behaved like a nineteen-year-old's whenever he was around her. There were times when all he could think about was making love to her, feeling that connection between their souls. Something about being inside her made him whole, and he couldn't get enough—especially without a latex barrier in the way.

Bracing an arm on the wall above her head, he leaned his forehead against hers. "Sometimes I think I need you *too* much, El, and that makes me lose my mind. I asked earlier what you saw in me because I don't get it. Where you see something that makes me worthy of your heart—which is bigger than the entire Rocky Mountain chain—I see a pushy dickhead, and that baffles me. I want to do right by you. So badly. I know I push too hard, but I never mean to drive you away. That's the last thing on this earth I want. I could spend the rest of my life looking for someone like you, and I'd come up empty ... and that's if I'm even *motivated* to look, which I wouldn't be because I think you need a heart to do that, and mine would be ripped from my body if I ever lost you."

Her eyes pooled. "Wow! That's quite the speech. You just blew my socks off, and I'm not even wearing any."

He chuckled mildly. "I guess being stuck in the cold and the dark opened up my eyes to a lot of things, and how much you own me is one of those things I'm coming to terms with. You could crush me so easily, El, and that's not easy to admit."

A single tear spilled down her pink cheek. She feathered her fingers across his heart. "Dave, you could never drive me away," she whispered. "I love you so, so much. I worry that *I'm* not good enough for *you*. Like with the baby. I'm so overwhelmed, especially when you're gone, and I feel inadequate, like I can't even hold up my end of the household. I don't want to disappoint you, but I-I worry that I'll be even worse with two, and then you'll see how bad I am at this, and *that* will disappoint *you*."

What? He gawked at her. "El, are you telling me you haven't wanted to have another kid because you're doing too much?"

She shrugged. "I guess I am. Lame, huh?"

"Hell no! Talk about stoic!" He shook his head. "Why didn't you say something before, Superwoman? You're so capable and independent, and nothing ever ruffles your feathers, so I never realized you might be struggling. You always make everything look like smooth sailing."

"I do?"

He lifted her wrist and placed a kiss in her palm. "Absolutely. But you know what? This is a problem I can fix. Let's hire people to help you. You can boss them around like you used to boss around your landscape crews." He winked, and relief flooded him when she laughed through her tears. "You may not know this, but I make a lot of money," he teased.

"Yes, you do make lots of money. But other wives are able to handle it all. I feel like something's wrong with me because I can't."

"Some do, El, but lots don't. Some have help without kids running around. Honestly, I've been wondering how you do it all. You cook, you clean, you take care of Kelsey, whether I'm there or not. Let's fix this. We'll worry about another baby later."

"Maybe sooner rather than later?" She broke into the sweet smile that never failed to melt his knees.

"I love you, Ellie, with all my heart. And if I'm being a dick and forget to tell you, kick me—just not in the jewels, okay?"

She trilled another laugh, making his blood fizz like the champagne in his glass. "*Never* there. They have a few more babies to make."

They joined the other guests in toasting the bride and groom, who, it turned out, were planning to "retire early." Dave couldn't take his eyes off Ellie, and he smiled inside as he watched her chat and smile with everyone. Goddamn, she was beautiful. Everything about her. And she was his, which made him one lucky fucker.

It had taken one near-death experience for him to realize what he'd known all along but had let slip away from him, that the gifts he'd been given were to be cherished forever. He'd never lose sight again.

The party was in full swing when Blake and Michaela made the rounds to thank their guests and say good night, taking a ribbing for cutting out early.

"Hey, my attorney wife insists we have some consummating to do or the ceremony we had today won't hold up in court," Barrett chuckled. "And no offense—we love you all—but to us, we're not leaving soon enough." When he began reciting trivia about wedding nights, Michaela tugged on his arm and led him away. The entire room cheered.

"They have the right idea," T.J. glanced at Natalie and looked at his watch. "The way I see it, we have exactly twelve hours to make up for the past three days. Looks like we'd better hustle if we're gonna make a baby."

"T.J., stop!" Laughing, she rested her hand on his chest, her eyes sparkling. She leaned in, going all conspiratorial, and he took the opportunity to breathe in the heady scent of vanilla and flowers. "I'm still on birth control, so it's going to take a while to finish my cycle and let my body adjust."

"Oh. Damn. I hadn't thought about that." He gave her a wicked smile. "I have this theory."

"Fascinated to hear it."

"If we want to make the perfect baby, we're going to have to practice ... a lot."

She let out a throaty chuckle. "We've *been* practicing a lot."

"Yeah, nah. There's room for improvement." When she cocked an eyebrow at him, he hurried on. "No improvement needed on your side. No, that's one hundred percent perfection. I'm talking about me. *I* need more practice." He paused a beat, rubbing his chin. "And you know what would really inspire me to be better?"

She gave him a sexy smirk. "Oh, pray tell what is going through that naughty mind of yours?"

"If you let me paint you … naked."

Her eyebrows slowly rose, kissing her hairline, and her smile broadened. "You're naked while you paint me? Oh, I love that idea!"

He rolled his eyes. "No, smartass. *You're* naked."

She shrugged a shoulder. "So Naked Day, but you're painting me?"

He grinned. "Something like that."

Her eyes traveled to the ceiling. "So are you *painting* me, as in you're making a portrait, or are you *painting* me, as in you're applying paint to my body with a variety of brushes?"

His dick sat up and looked around, pretty sure it was playtime. "Uh …"

She gave him a knowing smile. "Either scenario sounds … interesting."

Images of her rolling around in blobs of colorful paint, of him dabbing paint on every part of her body, had him yanking at his suddenly too-tight collar. He figured it was a better alternative to him yanking at the crotch of his suddenly too-tight pants. "Maybe we should blow this Popsicle stand and drive home early?"

Dropping her arms around his neck, she pushed up on her toes and hovered her mouth near his. His arms automatically wound around her, pulling her close. Liquid amber eyes pierced his. "Let's drive home tomorrow, like we planned, and spend the night in our fancy suite here instead. It's been a very long day, and we're both tired. Besides, my clothes are feeling a little …

snug. Maybe we should just retire now and you can help me out of them. What do you think?" She ghosted a kiss over his lips, a promise of so much more to come.

"No. Can. Think," he grunted in his best caveman. "Blood gone from brain."

With a soft tinkling laugh, she tugged on his tie and pulled him after her. "Follow me."

"Anywhere. Anytime. I'm all yours. Did I mention it's forever?"

"I think we sort of promised forever at our own wedding, didn't we?"

"Just wanted to remind you so you don't forget."

After she dragged him into their bedroom—willingly—he closed and locked the door, then set about reminding her of a few other things she would never forget.

Andie lay beside Beckett, auburn hair fanned across the white pillowcase in a sex-tousled riot. He sifted her silky waves between his fingers while her eyes scanned his face. *Afterglow. Haven't done this in a long, long time.*

"I wish Larry could have come to the wedding," she sighed. "I'd like to meet him in person sometime and thank him for giving me my husband back."

"So you're glad to have me back, huh?"

"Stop fishing. You know I am!" She whacked his arm playfully, then her expression grew serious. "Beck, I've been thinking."

He gave her a broad grin. "Uh-oh. Should I be worried?"

"I don't think so. It's just ... I realized a few things while you were lost."

He brushed a kiss across her forehead. "Such as?"

"Such as, you were right. I say one thing about family coming first, but I don't behave like that's true."

"Pixie, I don't—"

She pressed her forefinger to his lips and shushed him. "Just listen, okay? In my heart, I *am* a mom and wife first. Those are what matter most to me. But I've let my business run my life, and honestly, I haven't been happy about it. I have capable people working for me, and it's time I trusted them to take care of things when I'm not around. I want my real-life priorities to align with the ones in my heart."

He sighed and rolled onto his back. She moved with him, snuggling against his side, her hand over his heart. "I don't want you doing this because I'm being a selfish ass. I never should have said anything about you not being at my game. I knew you were there, I knew you were watching, but I got bent out of shape over our loss and decided to act like a dick to you. It wasn't fair. I want you to know, though, I love having you there."

"So you can show off your coaching skills?" He could hear the smile in her voice.

"Maybe, but mostly it's because I get a boost from it. And lately ..." Another sigh escaped him. "Lately, I need all the boost I can get because the games have been ugly, and I'm not sure how much longer I'll be there."

"You're not thinking they'll fire you, are you?"

He nodded, and a weight lifted from his shoulders unexpectedly. He'd admitted it. Out loud.

She propped her elbow and cradled her head in her palm. Her fingertips brushed over his skin as she spoke. "Beck, for someone who's building a program, I think you're being too hard on yourself. But let's say they do let you go. It'll sting, but we'll get through it. You've got me and the girls. I won't pretend it's the same as having a career, but we're your biggest fans, and we'll always be there." She laid her head on his chest and wrapped her arm around him. "I love you, Beck. I love you, and I believe in you. Always."

Tears gathered in his eyes and clogged his throat. He dug the heel of his palm into his eyes. "You're right that they're not the same, but I had a real epiphany out there: I never thought about the job. Not once. I thought about you, and I thought about the girls. *That's* what filled my mind, and possibly leaving you behind was what I regretted most. So I agree with you. If they can me, I might have to put my pride on IR, but that's nothing compared to what I have with my girls. You're all I need."

She lifted her head and parked her chin on his chest. "It was the lingerie, wasn't it?"

He barked out a confused laugh. "What?"

"The lingerie you gave me, that I wore tonight. I really rocked your world, didn't I, Tiger? Made you forget all about being a hockey coach. It was my plan all along." Her pale green eyes shone with mischief ... and so much love he nearly choked.

He pulled her to him and pecked her lips. "Yes, you little minx. That did it. Well, almost."

Her eyes widened. "Almost?"

"I need a little more convincing, so why don't you put on a few new pieces and do that little model-dance thing you did for me earlier? Not too many, though; I don't want to work very hard. I've just been through quite an ordeal."

"The old sympathy ploy, huh?"

"Any angle I can work."

She brushed her lips over his. "And you work those angles very, very well."

He pulled her back down flush against him, his eyes locked on hers. "On second thought, let's skip the lingerie."

Blake emerged in the kitchen with M in tow, pulling in the aromas of a Justin-made breakfast. His stomach rumbled its appreciation. Justin looked up and gave them a knowing grin. Blake didn't miss how his eyes widened for a beat when they landed on M. Blake glanced over his shoulder at her, and pride swelled in his chest. She was gorgeous, as always, but she had that well-fucked glow about her this morning that would make it hard to keep his eyes—and hands—off her for long.

"Where is everyone?" she asked as she slid onto a stool. Blake eased beside her, careful not to bump his sore hip.

"Believe it or not, you're the first ones up." Justin pulled a fresh pan of muffins from the oven. He looked around himself with a smug smile. "I'd say my work here is done."

M held up her hand to Blake. "And so is ours, apparently."

He high-fived her. "Yep, looks like our friends who needed to make it over the bumps did just that."

"And bumping is probably what's keeping them all from breakfast," M giggled.

"All it took was a wedding and a near-death experience," he chuckled.

"And the magic of the holiday season," she added. "Don't forget that."

He leaned in for a kiss. "Never."

Best. Christmas. Ever.

THE END

Want more Playmakers? Here you go!

HE'S BEEN BURNED by commitment. She can't seem to find the one. Here's an excerpt from *Besting the Blueliner*, Book 8:

It was no small surprise when an unfamiliar white pickup towing an empty trailer pulled up in front of Cam's house.

The second surprise came when the driver bounded from the vehicle carrying a load of something cloaked under a red-and-white-checkered cloth. It looked like a tablecloth his mother might spread over a picnic table. The stun factor had him rooted in place until a loud knock came at the front door, pulling him from his fog. Grace, who was far sharper than he this morning, already stood at the front door, inhaling the air in the crack between the door and frame.

Terra beamed from under a nylon hood when he opened the door. "Hi!" She pushed her way inside.

"Hi?" He suppressed the urge to ask what the hell she wanted, watching her back as she took a few more steps inside his house, her coat shedding raindrops all over his floor. Only Grace's greeting stopped Terra's advance, like an invisible force field. His dog wiggled from head to rear, her tail doing a fine imitation of a helicopter rotor. This was how she usually greeted *him*, not a sworn enemy. He needed to have a talk with his girl as soon as he could shoo the drippy one back out from where she had come from. "Can I help you?"

Terra pivoted and held out the checkered tablecloth to him. "I brought you something."

He arched a skeptical eyebrow. "Will it explode? Does it bite?"

Her face fell, and he instantly regretted his snark. She recovered quickly, flashing a smile as she whipped the tablecloth off of the bundle it cloaked. A tray of colorful cupcakes sat under a thin layer of clear plastic, perfectly swirled thick blue icing as high as the cake part with a perfect chocolate bean adorning it. They looked like the kind of treats that tempted him from his favorite bakery's case, and he realized too late he'd licked his bottom lip, giving himself away. If he stared much longer, he'd drool worse than Grace when bacon was on the menu.

Terra gave him a triumphant grin. "I took a chance you liked cupcakes, so I made these for you. They're chocolate with cherry filling."

Chocolate? With cherry filling? Well, shit! How had she zeroed in on his Achilles' Heel? His internal alarms sounded—she had to want something from him, like everyone else who ever offered him gifts, food or otherwise. "I thought you were afraid of Grace ... and maybe even me?" He cocked a questioning eyebrow at her.

"Having the great equalizer helps."

"The great what?"

She jerked her head to one side, and his gaze dropped to the sidearm barely concealed by her raincoat; he hadn't noticed it before.

Huh. "Yet you had the 'great equalizer' last time you were here, and you were still intimidated," he pointed out.

"I wasn't intimidated. I was simply ... frazzled." She patted the pistol. "I do know how to use it." Her sunny smile was completely at odds with her mildly veiled threat.

"As you should," he replied dryly. He pointed at the cupcakes. "What are they for?"

"For helping me yesterday." Her voice dropped. "And today." She thrust the tray at him, revealing his neatly folded flannel shirt beneath. "And I washed your shirt. Thanks for the loan."

He resisted the urge to shake his head and got to the important bit hiding in the unsolicited fanfare. "Today?"

"Um, yeah. I was hoping you could help me get the side-by-side on my trailer? Seeing as how you have those big muscles and all." Her eyes did some weird blinky thing he could only interpret as an attempt at Olympic eyelash-batting or clearing out a gnat that had splatted against one of her irises.

Relieving her of his shirt, he shoved the tray of cupcakes back at her. "I'm busy."

Those big blues of hers took a tour around the room before sweeping him from his bed head to his bare toes. "You don't *look* busy. What are you busy doing?"

His hackles, tempered by amusement at her boldness, rose. "Not sure that's any of your business." He took an extra loud slurp of his coffee. "Are you always this nosy?"

Grace, who had been sitting patiently beside him, cleaning the floor with her tail, lunged toward Terra—to get better acquainted, no doubt. Terra's eyes bugged, and she jumped backward with a squeak, smashing the back of her head into a hall tree too rickety to hold anything beyond a ball cap. She sent it and the tray crashing to the floor.

He wasn't sure where to turn his attention first: Terra's head, the toppled hall tree, or the cupcakes smearing his floor.

Get *Besting the Blueliner* at Amazon and find out what surprises are in store for Cam and Terra when they're thrown together in the isolated mountains of Colorado.

If you haven't already done so, sign up for my mailing list at www.gkbrady.com and be the first to learn about upcoming releases, cover reveals, and exclusive bonus content for subscribers only. I can't wait to connect with you!

Author's Note

Bringing the characters from Books 1 through 7 together for a holiday wedding was an absolute blast for me. I loved going back and visiting with all of them, and I hope you enjoy the result! If you haven't read any other books in The Playmakers Series® yet, you can dive in anywhere! While some of the characters make appearances in each other's stories, each book can be read as a standalone.

If this is your first read in the series, you'll get a peek into each Playmaker's personality and the dynamite woman at his side, and I hope you fall in love with them all.

And if you did enjoy the book, please consider leaving a review on Amazon, BookBub, or Goodreads to help readers like you find the story!

I barely scratched the surface of what Search and Rescue teams do and how vital they are. Complexity doesn't even begin to describe their world, and remember, they are volunteers. They don't get paid to go into the worst circumstances, under the worst conditions, to rescue people who have found themselves in the wrong place at the wrong time. They are true heroes and heroines, and my admiration for them grows exponentially every time I learn something new about them and their missions.

STAY UP TO date on more bonus content, new releases, discount deals, and giveaways by joining my mailing list at www.gkbrady.com. I can't wait to connect with you!

Acknowledgments

My heartfelt thanks to Carlos Espinosa of Chaffee County Search and Rescue for taking time to answer my questions and for sharing your vast knowledge about the complex world of search and rescue. I am in awe of the work you and your colleagues do and thank you for volunteering your time to perform the grueling job of finding people who need your brand of rescuing. And no offense, but I hope to never see you on the side of a mountain, unless it happens to be sitting by a fire sipping hot toddies. That sort of meeting will do nicely, thank you very much.

To Jenny Q, for your beautiful cover (it makes my heart happy), and for your awesome editing skills. Number ten!

To Judith at Word Servings, for teaching me how to count.

To Stephanie, for the awesome graphics and all the other wonderful things you do in between your heaps of everyday obligations.

To my husband, Tim, always, for your encouragement and willingness to listen and help me over a writing hump, and for giving me the male perspective. You are my co-conspirator, and I continue to learn so much from you. High-marking? Who knew!

Also by This Author

The Playmakers Series®

Book 0 - *Line Change*
Book 1 - *Taming Beckett*
Book 2 - *Third Man In*
Book 3 - *Gauging the Player*
Book 4 - *The Winning Score*
Book 5 - *Defending the Reaper*
Book 6 - *No Touch Zone*
Book 7 - *Twisted Wrister*
Book 8 - *Besting the Blueliner*
Book 9 - *Guarding the Crease*
Novella - *Love Rinkside*

The Fall River Series

Book 1 - *The Keeper*
Book 2 - *The Fixer*
Book 3 - *The Rescuer* (coming 2025)

About the Author

Since childhood, all sorts of stories and characters have lived in G.K. Brady's imagination, elbowing one another for attention, so she's thrilled (as are they) to be giving them their voice on the written page.

An award-winning writer of contemporary romance, she loves telling tales of the less-than-perfect hero or heroine who transforms with each turn of a page.

G.K. is a wife and the proud mom of three grown sons. She also writes historical fiction under the pen name Griffin Brady. She currently resides in Colorado with her very patient husband.

Connect with her on any of these platforms:

www.amazon.com/author/gkbrady

www.twitter.com/GKBrady_Writes

www.facebook.com/AuthorG.K.Brady/

www.bookbub.com/authors/g-k-brady

www.goodreads.com/author/show/19488321.G_K_Brady

www.instagram.com/authorg.k.brady

www.pinterest.com/gkbrady0993/